Heartland

Thicker Than Water

Heartland

Share every moment . . .

Coming Home

After the Storm

Breaking Free

Taking Chances

Come What May

One Day You'll Know

Out of the Darkness

Thicker Than Water

Heartland

❧

Thicker Than Water

by Lauren Brooke

SCHOLASTIC INC.

New York Toronto London Auckland Sydney
Mexico City New Delhi Hong Kong Buenos Aires

With special thanks to Linda Chapman

Library of Congress Cataloging-in-Publication data available.

ISBN 0-439-31715-0

Heartland series created by Working Partners Ltd, London.

Copyright © 2002 by Working Partners Ltd.
Published by Scholastic Inc. All rights reserved.

12 11 10 9 8 7 6 5 4 3 2 1   2 3 4 5 6 7/0
Printed in the U.S.A.   40
First Scholastic printing, May 2002

For Elaine

Chapter One

The Appaloosa filly snorted and threw her head high. Her eyes rolled. Every muscle in her body was tense.

"Easy now, Rosie," fifteen-year-old Amy Fleming murmured. Her right hand moved on the skin of the horse's neck in light circles. With each circle she made she breathed out softly. In her left hand she held a halter. From outside the stall came the everyday sounds of the busy boarding stables where Rosie was kept. Stable hands were calling to one another, horses were stamping their hooves and snorting, visitors were walking up and down the barn aisles, but Amy barely heard any of it. Her attention was riveted on the frightened filly.

"Be careful, Amy," Lou said from the stall door where she was standing with Sheri Hegland, Rosie's owner.

Amy could hear the anxiety in her sister's voice. She

1

nodded, but her determined gray eyes remained focused on the horse. "It's OK, girl," she whispered. "I'm not going to hurt you. I'm here to help."

"She's been like this ever since I bought her," Sheri said. "She just freaks every time I try to halter her. If you can't cure her, I don't know what I'm going to do."

"We'll do our best," Lou said.

"It must feel good, helping horses that have problems or have been abused," Sheri said. "It must be so fulfilling."

Amy heard Lou clear her throat rather awkwardly. "Actually, I don't really have much to do with the treatment of the horses myself. It's Amy and our stable hand, Ty, who do most of the work with the horses. I just help with the business side of things."

Not just, Amy corrected Lou in her mind. Heartland, the equine sanctuary founded by their mother, couldn't survive without someone managing the business side of things.

Amy focused on the filly again. Rosie's head had lowered, and she seemed to have relaxed slightly. Amy moved her hand toward the horse's ears, but as soon as she did so Rosie stiffened again. Moving her hand back, Amy contented herself with working some more on Rosie's neck. It looked like getting the halter on the filly was going to be a long, slow process, but if she had to take her time, then that's what she would do.

🙠

Ten minutes later Amy's fingers had finally reached the top of Rosie's neck. As her hand inched toward the filly's ears she noticed a long scar running down the outside of the left ear. What had caused it? An accident? Rough treatment?

"Do you know what might have caused this scar?" Amy asked Sheri.

"I'm afraid not," Sheri answered her. "I don't know that much about Rosie's history. I bought her as an unbroken three-year-old at a horse sale in Maryland. The guy selling her said he hadn't done anything with her apart from halter training her. He said she was quiet, but when I tried to halter her the next day she went crazy, rearing up and banging her head on the stall partition."

"Hmm." Amy looked thoughtful. Studying the scar on Rosie's ear, Amy felt sure that it had something to do with the way the filly was behaving. She scanned Rosie's face. Her head had lowered again, and she looked almost relaxed. It was time to get the halter on. Tightening her grip on it, Amy slipped it over the filly's nose.

Rosie immediately jerked her head up, but Amy was too quick for her. Flipping the headpiece behind the Appaloosa's ears, she fastened the buckle.

"Whoa there," she said to sooth the filly.

Rosie's muscles trembled, but at the touch of Amy's hand on her neck she slowly calmed down.

"Well done, Amy," Lou said in relief.

"She'll be OK now," Sheri said quickly. "It's just getting the halter on that causes it. That's why I didn't realize the problem until I got her home — she had the halter on all the time at the sale, and I didn't think to check to see if she'd let me take it on and off. If you hang on to her, I'll go get her travel wraps."

As Sheri hurried away down the barn aisle Amy reached around to tighten the scrunchy securing her light brown hair into a long ponytail. "Looks like we've got some work to do with you, girl," she said, scratching the Appaloosa affectionately on the neck.

Rosie snorted softly, calm now.

Lou came into the stall. With her short, golden hair, she and Amy looked very different. "I almost thought you weren't going to be able to get that halter on. You were so patient with her."

Hearing the admiration in her sister's voice, Amy shrugged. "It's just experience. Mom taught me everything before" — she struggled for a moment with the words — "before she died." It was almost eight months since their mom, Marion, had been killed in a road accident. The intense grief that Amy had felt right after the accident had diminished, but she carried with her a deep sense of loss that she knew would never fade.

Lou sighed. "I wish I were half as good with horses as you are."

There was a wistful note in her sister's voice that made Amy look at her with surprise. Since moving from Manhattan to Heartland, Lou had shied away from getting involved with the horses, except for Sugarfoot, a little Shetland. This was the first time Amy had heard Lou suggest that she would like things to be different.

"But you could be," Amy said to her. "You just need to spend more time with them. If you want, I could teach you everything Mom taught me."

"Really?" For a moment, Lou looked almost tempted. "I'm not sure I have what it takes. It seems like it's second nature for you and Ty."

"That's not true!" Amy said. "You would be great. Just think about Sugarfoot. You're the reason he got better." Amy knew Lou's bond with the pony was what helped him pull through his sickness the year before. "It would be cool, Lou. We could work together." She glanced at her sister's face and saw a sudden look of excitement there. "Why not?"

Just then Sheri came to the doorway. "Here are the wraps and her tail bandage. Do you want me to put them on?"

Sheri's appearance shattered the intimacy of the moment. In the blink of an eye the eagerness left Lou's face, and her expression became cool and composed once more.

"Thanks, Sheri," she replied briskly. "I'll go and lower the ramp on the trailer. When Rosie's ready, bring her around to the parking lot."

"Hey, Lou, what about what we were just discussing?" Amy protested.

Lou's eyes seemed to slip away from hers. "Maybe it's better if I just stick to what I know best," she said quietly, and with that she walked off.

Sheri looked a bit confused. "Sorry — did I interrupt something?" she asked, watching Lou go.

"It's OK," Amy replied. She stared after Lou for a moment and then brought her mind back to the job at hand. "Let's get Rosie ready."

Taking the tail bandage from Sheri, she began to wrap it around Rosie's tail.

If only Lou would help with the horses more, Amy thought as Sheri began to put the leg protectors on. *Then maybe we'd get along better. We might even go out riding together. . . .*

Amy caught her thoughts. It wasn't very likely. After all, Lou hadn't ridden for more than twelve years.

She tied up the bandage and saw that Sheri had just put on the last leg wrap and was straightening up. Amy fixed a smile on her face. "OK," she said, patting Rosie's hindquarters. "Looks like she's ready to go."

❧

The Heartland trailer stood in the large parking lot. Tall Oaks, the boarding barn where Rosie was stabled, had more than seventy stalls. Around the parking lot, the paddocks stretched out in all directions, and to the left were three training rings.

Rosie loaded easily into the trailer. Apart from being head shy, she didn't seem to be a particularly nervous horse. *Quiet and reserved, maybe,* Amy thought as she tied her up, *but not nervous.*

"We'll give you a call tonight and let you know how she's settling in," Lou told Sheri as they fastened the bolts holding the ramp up. "And of course, feel free to visit any time you want."

"Thanks," Sheri said. "I sure hope you can help her." She went around to the side door and gave Rosie a last pat. "You be good now, girl."

Rosie whinnied in reply.

Lou fastened the door and turned to Amy. "I'll be right back. I just want to take some of our brochures to the office," she said. "Maybe we'll get some more business from here."

Amy nodded. Creating brochures advertising Heartland's services had been Lou's idea. She dropped them off wherever she could — tack stores, grain merchants, boarding stables like this one. So far the leaflets had gen-

erated a fair amount of business, and Amy, who had orig-
inally been opposed to the idea, had to admit that maybe
they were a good move after all — just like Lou's idea for
a fund-raising barn dance and an open house to show off
the techniques that Heartland used to heal horses.

But not all of Lou's ideas had worked, Amy thought. Sometimes her sister got so caught up in making money that
she seemed to forget that Heartland was more than just
a business — it was about living, breathing horses.

Amy glanced at her watch. How long was Lou going
to be? She wandered up the yard, past the barns, toward
the three training rings. There was just one rider out, a
girl younger than Amy, who was trotting a rose-gray
Arabian pony around the ring. The pony looked tense,
and as Amy approached he slowed to a stop. Tossing his
head, he tried to pull toward the gate. But the girl was
clearly a good rider. Sitting deep in her saddle, she urged
him on.

Amy recognized her. Her name was Jo-Ann Newhart,
and she attended the same elementary school that Amy
had. She must be in about sixth grade now, Amy
thought, watching as the younger girl refused to let her
pony get away with breaking for the gate.

"Please be careful, honey," a woman watching at the
fence called out to the girl. "I think you ought to bring
him in. He doesn't look too happy."

"He's fine, Mom!" Jo-Ann said swiftly. "Go on,

Feather!" she exclaimed as the gray pony stopped again. Although her riding position was good, her shoulders looked hunched up and tense. She kicked Feather on, glancing nervously at her mom as she did so.

The pony's hooves were defiantly squared. He seemed determined not to move. Shaking his head, he began to back up. Jo-Ann clicked her tongue and kicked his sides, but he kept going backward. Jo-Ann turned him in a circle, and he stopped dead.

"OK, that's enough," Mrs. Newhart said, her voice high and anxious. "I want you to bring him in now, Jo-Ann."

"No," Jo-Ann said, and Amy thought she heard a note of desperation in the younger girl's voice. Bringing her whip down, Jo-Ann smacked Feather on his shoulder. Amy saw the pony sink down on his hocks.

"Watch out!" she gasped instinctively, but it was too late. Feather had reared into the air.

Mrs. Newhart screamed as Jo-Ann threw herself forward on Feather's neck when he came down.

"Turn him in a circle!" Amy shouted above the sound of Mrs. Newhart's gasps and screams. Amy scrambled over the gate, wondering wildly if she could somehow grab the pony's reins before he went up again. But before she could reach him, Jo had done what Amy had said. Throwing her weight to one side, she pulled the pony's head and neck around in as tight a circle as possible. Thrown off balance, there was no way that Feather could rear again.

"Are you OK?" Amy demanded, grabbing the pony's reins before he decided to try anything else.

Jo's face was white with shock, but she nodded at Amy. "I'm — I'm fine."

"Jo-Ann! Get off that animal right now!"

Amy and Jo glanced around. Mrs. Newhart was fumbling with the gate.

"I'm OK, Mom," Jo protested.

"Now, Jo-Ann!"

Looking very reluctant, Jo threw one leg over the saddle and slid off Feather's back. Mrs. Newhart got the gate open and came running across the ring toward her. "That's the last straw," she said, her voice shaking. "That pony's dangerous. He's unpredictable. Your uncle should never have bought him for you!"

"It's fine, Mom. I'm all right," Jo insisted.

"This time," her mother replied, "but what about next time?" She shook her head. "I'm sorry, honey. We've got to get rid of him. I can't have you risking your life like this."

"Mom!" Jo exclaimed.

Mrs. Newhart looked like she was about to take Feather's reins from Jo, but then she seemed to think better of it. She suddenly seemed to notice Amy. "Thanks for helping," she said quickly. "Can you give

Jo-Ann a hand putting Feather back in the barn? I don't think she should lead him on her own." It was obvious that she thought Amy worked at Tall Oaks.

Amy didn't bother to tell her that she didn't. "Sure," she said, looking sympathetically at Jo.

"I don't need any help, thank you," Jo said angrily. "Feather and I will be just fine." Grabbing Feather's reins, she began to march toward the gate, but before she went Amy caught a glimpse of tears welling up in her hazel eyes.

"I'm going to wait in the car," Mrs. Newhart called after her. "I expect you to be there in five minutes. Is that clear?"

Jo nodded briefly and led Feather out of the ring.

Amy hurried after her. "Are you OK?"

Jo stopped dead. "OK?" she exclaimed. "How could I be OK? My mom's going to sell Feather!" Her angry words hung in the air. A look of contrition fell across her face. "Sorry," she said. "I didn't mean to get mad. It's not your fault. It's hers. It's totally unfair." She swallowed and led Feather forward.

Amy felt desperately sorry for her. "Your mom's just worried, Jo," she said, following her. "Rearing is dangerous. If Feather fell over on you he could break your back. Maybe it would be better if you did get another pony."

"You don't understand," Jo said, one hand gripping Feather's mane. "I won't get another one. Mom didn't want me to have Feather in the first place. My uncle bought him for me, and now that this has happened Mom won't let me have another pony. I'll be lucky if I'm allowed to ride at all. She doesn't trust horses — she never has."

Amy was shocked.

"It's so unfair," Jo went on as she led Feather into his stall. "Feather's not dangerous. I mean, he has his crazy days — usually when Mom happens to be watching — but he's only reared a couple of times before." Feather rubbed his gray head against her chest and snorted happily.

Amy frowned. Her own mom had always said that you could analyze a horse's personality by looking at its face, and looking at Feather she thought that the shape of his face backed up what Jo had said. He had large, almond-shaped eyes, normally the sign of a gentle, soft-natured horse. He was an Arabian, and his dished face, fluted ears, and complex, wrinkled chin suggested that he was likely to have an extremely sensitive, cooperative character. Feather definitely didn't look mean, stubborn, or resistant.

"He's only reared a couple of times?" she said.

Jo nodded. "Yes. Like I said, most of the time he's perfect."

Amy frowned, and after offering her hand to the pony to sniff, she started to feel along his back and neck with her hands. "Maybe he's sore someplace," she said to Jo. "He could have a pulled muscle in his back or something."

Suddenly, a light seem to come on in Jo's eyes.

"Amy!" she said. "You know all about horses with problems, don't you? You can help me! Mom would have to let me keep him if you said you could cure him. If he's only rearing because he's hurt, we just have to make him better. You could take him to your stable to work with him, and then . . ."

"Whoa!" Amy interrupted her. "Even if Feather comes to Heartland, there's no guarantee that we can help him. Rearers are dangerous. You need to realize that." She saw Jo's face fall. "But I guess there is a small chance that we can help," she said quickly. "If there's a genuine reason for him rearing — like pain — then maybe we can cure him, especially since his rearing hasn't become an established habit."

"Oh, Amy, it would mean so much to me if you'd try to help him." Jo looked beseechingly at her.

"OK," Amy said. "I'll try."

"Thank you!" Jo exclaimed. "Oh," she said suddenly. "How am I going to convince Mom? She still wants to sell him."

"Let's get my sister, Lou," Amy said quickly. "She's really good at persuading people. Maybe if we talked to your mom together we might get her to let Feather come to Heartland."

She jogged back to the trailer.

Lou was waiting there. "I was beginning to get worried about you," she said.

"Lou, I need to talk to you." Seeing Mrs. Newhart sitting in a car nearby, Amy pulled Lou around to the far side of the trailer and explained the situation with Feather.

"I think there's a chance we could help him — at least I'd like to give it a try," she said. "We've got an empty stall now that Gallant Prince has gone."

Lou looked concerned.

"Feather's only reared a couple of times," Amy went on. "And there might be a genuine reason for his behavior — he could be afraid or in pain. If we can figure out what it is, then his rearing should stop."

Lou still looked worried. "But rearing is one of the hardest things to treat. I'm sure I remember Mom once saying that there's no safe way to deal with a rearing horse."

"I'll be careful," Amy said. "I've got to at least try. Jo is so upset."

Lou hesitated for a moment. "OK," she said at last, although her eyes were reluctant. "Let's go and get him."

Amy took a deep breath. "There's one little problem."

Lou looked at her questioningly.

"Jo's mom," Amy admitted.

🙰

To Amy's relief, Lou agreed to help her persuade Mrs. Newhart to allow Feather to go to Heartland.

"There's a good chance we can help him," Lou said to Mrs. Newhart as she and Amy explained Jo's idea. "Amy and Ty are both very experienced in dealing with problem horses."

"Please say yes," Jo begged her mom. "It'll be perfect. Heartland's close to our house, and I'll be able to see him regularly."

Mrs. Newhart looked worried. "I'm really not sure."

"Even if you just let us have him for a few weeks," Lou said, "let's see if we can help him."

"Please, Mom," Jo said. "You can't sell him without giving him a second chance."

"All right," Mrs. Newhart agreed reluctantly. "He can go to Heartland for one month." Jo's face lit up. "But if he isn't cured within that time, then we are selling him," she added firmly. "And you're not allowed to ride him until I'm sure he's safe, Jo."

"I won't," Jo promised. She hugged her mom. "Thanks, Mom."

Amy felt a mixture of relief and anxiety. One month wasn't long. What if they couldn't help him in that time?

"You need to tell me everything you know about his

past," she said to Jo as they went to Feather's stall to get him ready to travel. "It might help me figure out what's making him act up. Has he been moved around a lot? Has he had lots of owners? Things like that can often unsettle a horse."

"But that hasn't happened to Feather," Jo said. "My uncle bought him from a family he knew in Maryland. They'd had him for five years and were only selling him because the youngest daughter had outgrown him. They bought him from his breeder when he was four years old. She showed him in conformation classes."

Amy frowned. "So there's never been any hint of bad behavior before?"

"No," Jo said. "And he's almost always really good with me. It's just sometimes that he goes crazy." She looked at Amy. "You *will* be able to help him, won't you?" she said anxiously.

"I'll try my best," Amy promised her. "I really will."

Feather loaded easily into the trailer. He sniffed noses with Rosie and then nuzzled Jo. "I'll come to visit you tomorrow, baby," she promised, kissing his muzzle. Her voice dropped to a whisper. "I love you."

Amy smiled. Because Jo was several years younger, she hadn't really seen much of her at school. Even though she had only seen her for a short time that day, she was already beginning to like her.

I just hope I can help her and Feather, she thought as Jo jumped out of the trailer, her dark-red hair bouncing on her shoulders.

"I'll see you tomorrow, Amy," Jo called.

"Yeah, see you!" Amy smiled. She got into the pickup beside Lou.

Lou raised her eyebrows as Amy shut the door. "Now you're sure there are no other horses that you want us to squeeze in while we're at it?" she teased.

"Well, there is some space in the tack compartment," Amy said, pretending to consider Lou's question seriously. "I suppose I could always go and see if I can find a little pony." She put her hand on the door handle.

Lou quickly started the engine. "Too late!" she said, putting her foot down on the gas pedal and smiling. "Which is probably just as well. I'm already wondering what Ty will say when we get back!"

Amy grinned. That was true. What would Ty say when they unloaded not one horse but two!

Chapter Two

"Amy!" Ty exclaimed as Amy lowered the trailer ramp to the ground. "There's another horse in there!"

Amy pretended astonishment. "Gee!" she said, looking at him innocently. "How did that get in there?"

Ty shook his head at her, a smile tugging at the corners of his determined mouth. "OK — explain."

"He reared with his owner, Jo, while I was watching, and her mom wanted to sell him on the spot," Amy said. She saw Ty's face start to crease into a frown. "I had to help."

"But a rearer —" Ty began, raking a hand through his dark hair.

"I know they're difficult, but he's only reared a couple of times before," Amy said. "Just take a look at him, Ty," she said, seeing the concern in Ty's eyes. "He's not mean, you can tell he's not."

Ty's green eyes held hers for a moment, and Amy felt her stomach turn a familiar somersault. She and Ty weren't exactly dating, but at Christmastime he had kissed her, and sometimes all it took was one look to bring the memory of that moment flooding back.

"I'll — I'll get him out," she said hastily, painfully aware of the blood that had flamed into her cheeks. "Then you can see what you think."

Ducking her head to hide her embarrassment, she went around to the side door. Rosie, the Appaloosa, was standing quietly, her head lowered, her eyes half closed. Giving her a quick pat, Amy untied Feather's lead rope and backed him out of the trailer.

Feather pranced out, his head high. As soon as his hooves hit the gravel, he swung around, his eyes darting across to the turnout paddocks on either side of Heartland's long driveway and then around to the old brick stables that stood at a right angle to the white, weatherboarded farmhouse.

With a snort, the gray pony lifted his front leg and began to paw at the gravel with a quick, sharp movement of his hoof.

"Steady, fella," Ty said, patting him. "He seems spirited," he commented. "Not a novice's pony."

Amy nodded. "Yeah, but Jo's a good rider. She's got a great seat. She stayed on him with no problem when he went up in the air." She glanced at Ty. He was studying the pony's fine-boned face. "So what do you think?" she said.

"Sensitive, gentle," Ty said, his eyes scanning Feather's delicate ears, large eyes, and small muzzle. "The sort of horse that might panic if he's scared or in pain." He turned and nodded. "Yeah, you did the right thing. Maybe there is a problem with him that we can solve. He sure doesn't look mean."

Amy felt a rush of relief. It was good to have Ty agree with her. He'd been working at Heartland since he was fifteen, just on weekends and during vacations at first, but when he was sixteen he'd left school, and her mom had offered him a full-time job. Marion had always said that he was a natural with horses.

"First thing we need to do," Ty continued, "is to get Scott to check him over. Maybe he has an injury that's making him irritable."

Amy nodded. Scott Trewin was the local equine vet. "And if there's no injury?"

"We take it from there," Ty finished.

They smiled at each other, and Amy felt a glow of contentment. She and Ty worked so well together it was like they could read each other's thoughts.

"Here," Ty said, holding out his hand. "I'll put him

away in Gallant Prince's old stall if you unload the filly. I've bedded down the stall next to Jake's for her."

"Thanks," Amy said, handing the lead rope over.

She ducked under the breast bar of the trailer and began to untie Rosie. The gentle Appaloosa rubbed her head against Amy's arm.

"You're a sweet girl, aren't you," Amy murmured, stroking Rosie's chestnut-and-white-flecked neck. "Come on, let's put you in your new stall." With a slight toss of her head, Rosie backed obediently out of the trailer and followed Amy.

Amy was just pushing the bolt across the white-painted stable door when she heard a clatter of hooves. She looked around. Ben Stillman, Heartland's newest stable hand, was riding his chestnut jumper, Red, in from the trails.

"Hi, there!" he greeted her. "Is that the new horse?" He nodded to Rosie, who was rubbing the side of her head along the top of the half door.

Amy nodded. "One of them." She saw Ben's inquiring look and shook her head. "It's a long story, but there's another in the back barn in Prince's old stall."

Ben raised his eyebrows. "I'll untack Red, and you can tell me all about it."

Amy clipped Rosie's lead rope to the hook outside the

stall door and followed Ben to Red's stall, two doors down. Ben had come to work at Heartland a few months earlier. Although it had taken a while for him to settle in, he was now definitely part of Heartland's extended family.

"So come on, what's the story?" Ben said as Amy appeared in the doorway.

Amy bent down and began to help take off Red's brushing boots. As she did so, she told Ben all about Jo and Feather. "I had to say we'd help," she finished.

"Of course you did," Ben said, his eyes concerned. "Poor kid. I bet she was really upset."

Amy nodded. "I just hope we can cure him."

"If anyone can, it's you and Ty," Ben said.

Amy felt a warm glow. "And you," she said, smiling at him. She patted Red. "How was he today?"

"Jumping out of his skin — in a good way," Ben said with a smirk. "There's an indoor training show at Willow Creek on Sunday that I think I might go to. Do you want to come? They've got junior jumpers — you could bring Sundance."

"Yeah!" Amy said immediately. Sundance, her pony, was an excellent jumper. He'd won Large Pony Champion several times, and for a while now Amy had been wanting to try him in the jumper division. The problem was that she was always so busy at Heartland, and there was hardly ever anyone free to take her to shows.

"I'll need to get some practice in," Amy said, quickly

trying to figure out when she would have the time. The February nights closed in really early. But maybe if she rode him before school, she could —

"Oh," she said suddenly as a thought struck her. "When did you say the show was?"

"This Sunday."

Amy's heart sank. "Then it's no good. I can't go."

"Why not?" Ben asked.

"My" — Amy's throat felt suddenly dry as she struggled over the word — "my father's visiting this weekend."

Ben's eyes leaped to her face. "Your father?" he echoed.

"Lou arranged it," Amy said. She fought down a faint flicker of excitement. She was not going to feel any emotion over the visit of the man who had deserted her, Lou, and their mom more than twelve years ago. After all, he'd never even tried to get in touch until last year. She corrected herself as the memory of a letter sent five years ago forced its way into her mind. In the letter he had begged her mom for a reconciliation. *But he didn't really try,* Amy thought angrily. *He could have written again. He could have come to see her in person.*

A defiant look lit up her gray eyes. "Maybe I'll come anyway," she declared. "I can always see him when I get back in the evening." She tilted her chin. "In fact, the less time I spend with him the better."

"But you haven't seen him for twelve years, Amy," Ben protested.

"So?" Amy shrugged, doing her best to ignore the little voice in her mind that insisted *What do you mean "so?" He's your father!* "It doesn't mean I have to spend all day with him. No, I'll come to the show with you."

"Oh, no, you won't," Ben said. "I wouldn't have asked you if I'd known your dad was visiting." Amy opened her mouth to object, but he cut in before she could speak. "Come on, Amy, I know more than anyone how important it is to work things out with your parents, even if you don't want to."

"But —" Amy began.

Ben shook his head. "You know I missed out on a lot by cutting my mom out of my life for six years. Give your dad a chance. If you don't, you'll be the one on the losing end."

Amy looked at him mutinously, but deep down she knew he was right. And anyway, there was Lou to think about, too. This visit meant an awful lot to her. For years she'd lived in hope of their father returning. She would go crazy if Amy went to a show the very weekend their father was here. "OK," she sighed. "I guess I can go to the next show with you."

Ben smiled at her. "Of course you can." Slinging Red's saddle and bridle over his arm, he walked to the door. "It's the best thing to do, Amy. You know it is."

"Yeah, right," Amy muttered.

Kicking a few loose stones, she walked to the back barn to find Ty.

If only her dad wasn't coming to visit. She, Lou, and Grandpa had their own life without him. Why couldn't he just stay in Australia with his new wife, Helena, and their baby girl?

As she walked through the barn door, several horses whinnied. Despite feeling cranky, Amy couldn't help but smile. That was the best thing about horses. You just couldn't stay in a bad mood when you were around them.

Giving out pats and horse cookies, she stopped briefly at each of the stalls that lined the wide concrete aisle.

"Hey, there," Ty said, looking out over Feather's stall door when Amy reached Sugarfoot's stall.

"Hi," Amy said as the little Shetland poked his nose up to the stall door and nuzzled her hands for cookies, his dark eyes peeking out from under his thick flaxen forelock.

Ty seemed to hear the faint sigh in her voice. He frowned. "What's wrong?"

"Nothing," Amy muttered. She fed Sugarfoot a final cookie and went into Feather's stall.

Ty's frown deepened. "Something's the matter. What's up?"

Amy saw the concern in his eyes, and suddenly everything came rushing out. "It's my dad's visit. I don't want him to come here, Ty. I don't want to see him at all."

Ty walked over. "Hey," he said softly, putting his hand on her shoulder. "I know it's going to be tough, but think of it this way — by meeting him you can finally come to terms with the past. You can put all that behind you."

Amy lifted her eyes to his.

"You only have to do it this once," Ty went on. "If you don't like him, then you don't have to see him again."

"I guess so," Amy grimaced. "I just wish I didn't have to meet him even once."

"I don't think you can avoid that," Ty said, drawing her close. "Come on. It'll be OK."

Just as Amy began to lower her head on Ty's shoulder for comfort, she heard Ben whistling as he walked into the barn. Amy pulled away guiltily. No one, apart from Soraya, Amy's best friend, had any idea that they were any more than just good friends. And that was the way Amy wanted to keep it. Until they decided exactly where their new relationship was going, she wanted as few people as possible to know. It was less complicated that way.

"Hi," Ben called, coming over to the stall. "So this is the other new pony," he said, looking at Feather, who was pulling quickly and nervously at his hay net.

"Yes," Amy said, hoping he wouldn't notice her confusion.

"Nice conformation," Ben commented. "Polish bloodlines, I'd say by the look of him." Ben had spent most of the last six years of his life on his aunt's Arabian stud farm, and he knew far more than Amy did about Arabians. "Do you know anything about his history?"

"Only a little," Amy said.

"Do you know what made him go up today?" Ben mused.

"That's what we've got to find out," Ty said. "Then maybe we can help him."

Amy looked at the pretty gray pony with the chestnut flecks in his coat and silvery mane and tail. Ty was right. Until they found the reason for his behavior, they wouldn't be able to help. And she desperately wanted to help him, as much for his sake as for Jo's.

🙢

At the end of the day, after the horses had been fed, the stalls mucked out, and the water buckets checked, Amy waved to Ty and Ben and trudged wearily to the house.

She walked into the warm kitchen. A beef stew was bubbling on the stove, and Lou was leaning against the sink, talking on the phone. Amy shrugged off her barn jacket and slung it over the back of one of the chairs. Lou automatically reached out and snagged it, moving it to the new coat rack that she had recently installed on the back of the kitchen door.

"OK, I better go," she said into the phone. "See you tomorrow."

"Scott?" Amy mouthed to Lou.

Lou nodded.

"Can I speak to him?" Amy said.

Lou nodded again. "Amy's here, Scott. She wants to talk to you." There was a pause and then, "Yeah, me, too," Lou murmured softly into the phone.

Amy grinned. A few months back, Scott and Lou had started dating. Judging by the sappy look in her sister's blue eyes, things still seemed to be going well.

Seeing her grin, Lou blushed and hurriedly held out the phone.

"Hi, Scott," Amy said.

"Amy!" Scott's warm voice greeted her. "What can I do for you?"

Amy explained about Feather. "Can you check him out for us?"

"No problem," Scott replied. "I'll stop by tomorrow morning about ten. And how's your newest rescue doing — that paint pony, Jigsaw?"

Amy thought about black-and-white Jigsaw. He had been a riding-school pony until he'd developed a stress fracture in one of his front legs from overwork. Unable to work the long days anymore, he'd been sent to a sale. He'd been about to go for glue when a former student from the riding school had spotted him. Out of pity, she bought him and then contacted Heartland to ask if they would take him in. Amy and Ty had immediately agreed.

"He's doing OK," Amy told Scott. "We've got him on cod liver oil and alfalfa cubes to help increase his calcium, as well as thirty leaves and one cleaned root of white comfrey a day. I read that comfrey's great for treating bone damage."

"Yes, I remember your mom using it once on a horse with a pelvic stress fracture," Scott said. "A bay hunter."

"Arctic," Amy said, remembering. She never forgot any horse that had been to Heartland. "It took him about three months to heal."

"Let's hope Jigsaw's as lucky," Scott said. "I'll stop by his stall when I'm visiting tomorrow."

As Amy put the phone down she found herself thinking how lucky they were to have Scott. Many vets ridiculed the types of treatments they used at Heartland, but Scott had always been interested in them. If it works, his attitude was, then why not do it? Amy only wished that more people in the horse world could be as open-minded.

"Where's Grandpa?" she asked, going to help Lou set the table.

"Taking a shower," Lou said. "He said supper should be ready in about ten minutes."

"Good. I'm starving!" Amy said.

Ten minutes later, Jack Bartlett, the girls' grandfather, came into the kitchen. "Ready to eat, you two?" he said, rubbing his hands.

"Definitely," Amy said, jumping to her feet and carrying over three plates.

Jack ladled out the Irish stew. He was a fantastic cook. For as long as Amy could remember, he had looked after the house and seen to the family's meals. Most of the time he left the horses to Amy and Ty, but when necessary, he put to use the various skills he had learned as a cattle farmer before he retired.

They sat down at the table. Lou picked up her knife and fork and then suddenly put them down again. "I wasn't going to tell you this yet," she said, a smile breaking out on her face, "but I just can't keep it to myself. I've had a great idea for a way to increase Heartland's revenue."

"Really? What is it?" Amy said, looking at her with interest.

Lou grinned. "I'm not telling yet. I want to find out if it's really possible first. I've arranged a meeting in town on Monday to check some things out. I'll tell you after that."

"At least give us a clue, Lou," Grandpa said.

Lou shook her head. "You'll have to wait till Monday. But believe me, it's a great idea. You'll love it." Her eyes shone happily. "If it works out the way I think, we'll be able to tell Daddy about it next weekend and see what he thinks."

Amy glanced at Grandpa. She knew he had never forgiven their father for abandoning them. His jaw tightened, but he seemed to control his feelings. "What time's your father coming on Saturday, Lou?" he asked.

"About ten o'clock," Lou said. "I can't wait, can you, Amy?"

Amy made herself smile. She knew how much this visit meant to Lou, and she wasn't going to let her own feelings spoil it. "No, it'll be good," she managed.

"I think I might go out for the day," Grandpa said.

"Go out?" Amy echoed, looking at him in alarm. It was going to be bad enough meeting their dad, but to do it without Grandpa there! How could he? She needed him for moral support.

"It's for the best," Grandpa said quietly.

Lou looked at him for a moment, but then she nodded as if she realized how much of a concession he was already making in letting Tim, their father, visit Heartland at all. "OK," she said. "I understand. And we both appreciate you letting Daddy come here, don't we, Amy?"

No, we don't, Amy wanted to argue. *Why couldn't you just have said no, Grandpa?* But she forced herself to smile. "Yeah. Thanks, Grandpa," she said, hoping her voice didn't sound as high and false to Lou as it did to her.

🙐

When Amy went up to her bedroom that night, she took along an old photo album. In it were snapshots of the family before Tim's accident — the accident at the

Show-jumping World Championships that had left him too badly injured to ever ride professionally again. It had been after his accident that he had abandoned his family. After facing up to the fact that he wasn't coming back, Marion reluctantly sold everything in England and returned to her childhood home in Virginia with three-year-old Amy. Lou, eleven at the time, had begged to be allowed to stay at her English boarding school, believing that one day her father would return for her.

Amy turned the pages of the album. One photo in particular caught her eye. It showed Lou and herself mounted on two ponies. Amy studied it. There she was, a skinny three-year-old with jodhpurs that were way too big for her, and there was eleven-year-old Lou, her blond hair in two chunky braids, grinning from ear to ear as she clutched a silver trophy.

Amy looked at the joy and happiness on her sister's face. It seemed almost unbelievable that the girl in the picture could have grown up into her serious, reserved sister. And she was riding a pony and looking so natural and at ease on him. It was like looking at a different person.

Amy's eyes moved to her parents. Marion stood beside Amy's pony, an arm flung casually around its neck, fair hair blowing in the breeze, mouth and eyes laughing. A stab of grief shot through Amy, and as tears blurred her vision she quickly looked away from the picture of her mom to where her dad was standing. Tall and dark-haired, he was smiling at Lou with a look of utter pride.

Amy swallowed. He looked so handsome, strong, and happy in the photo. *He sure has changed*, she thought, remembering the day last November when she had caught a brief glimpse of a tired middle-aged man at her mom's grave.

She shook her head. What would it be like meeting him again? What would she say to him?

A knock on the bedroom door startled Amy out of her thoughts.

"It's just me," Lou said, opening the door. "I'm going to make myself some hot chocolate. Do you want a cup?" Before Amy could answer, she saw the photo album on Amy's knee. "You've got Mom's old photos out," she said, walking over.

Amy nodded.

Lou looked at the photographs.

"Do you remember that day?" Amy asked, pointing at the photograph of the two of them on ponies.

Lou nodded. "I'd just won an equitation Jumping class. I remember being so glad that Daddy had been watching. I was determined I was going to be a show jumper just like him when I grew up."

"You look so happy," Amy said.

Lou nodded slowly. "I do, don't I?" she said at last.

She shook her head. "Things used to be pretty simple back then," she said quietly.

Hearing a strange note in her sister's voice, Amy glanced at her. There was a look in her eyes that was hard to define. Was it sadness, pain, loss? But before Amy had a chance to work it out, Lou had straightened up, the expression erased from her face.

"So do you want some hot chocolate?" she asked abruptly.

"Uh, no, thanks," Amy replied, taken aback by the sudden change in her.

"OK. Good night then," Lou said briskly. "See you in the morning."

Amy watched her sister leave the room.

As the door shut she found herself wondering what exactly she had seen in Lou's eyes. It had been more than just sadness. Had there also been a look of — she searched for the right emotion — regret?

Chapter Three

At ten o'clock the next morning, Scott Trewin's blue Jeep came bouncing up the driveway.

"Thanks for coming," Amy said as he parked and got out. There weren't many vets who would make a routine visit on a Sunday, but Scott was amazing. He never seemed to mind the hours he spent with horses.

"No problem," he said, smiling warmly. "I'm on call anyway. So where's this new pony you want me to look over?"

"In the barn," Amy said.

Just then the back door opened and Lou appeared. "Hey, there!" she said, walking over with a smile. "Amy said you were coming."

They kissed, and then Scott grinned at Amy. "See, maybe I do have another reason for dropping by!" He looked at Lou. "Are you coming up to the barn with us?"

Lou nodded, and they started to walk up the yard. Scott caught sight of Rosie, resting her head over her stall door. "Another new one?" he said.

"Yeah." Amy told him about Rosie's head shyness. "She just won't let you put anything near her ears. She's got a scar on one of them, so I'm figuring she had a bad experience in the past."

"Do you want me to look her over while I'm here?" Scott volunteered.

"That's OK," Amy said, not wanting to use up any more of Scott's precious free time. "Her owner got her checked out by her own vet before she contacted us. He didn't find anything wrong with her, though he had to sedate her to get close to her head."

They passed Ben, who was sweeping the feed room. He called out a greeting to Scott but didn't stop working. It was Ty's day off, and as usual when someone had a day off, there was a rush to get everything done.

Feather was looking over his stall door, his ears pricked, his eyes flickering from side to side.

"It's OK, fella. Easy now," Scott said, taking Feather's halter off the hook outside his stall and walking in.

Amy held Feather while Scott began to examine him. After listening to Feather's heart and lungs and checking his teeth, Scott felt carefully over the gray pony's body, starting at the top of his neck and working down methodically over his withers, back, and loins.

"Well, there's no obvious soreness," Scott said to Amy and Lou, "but let's take him out so I can see him move."

Amy led Feather out of the barn and trotted him up and down on the concrete so that Scott could check the pony for any lameness. Feather had the beautiful action typical of an Arabian, and he floated across the ground. Amy could certainly believe that he'd won ribbons in conformation classes.

"Well, he looks sound," Scott said. "Just hold him still for me on that piece of level ground, Amy."

Amy did as he asked, and Scott examined the pony from all angles, searching for any signs of unevenness in his body that could have suggested that Feather had a physical problem. But at the end of the examination, Scott shook his head and patted the pony. "Perfect — or as near as can be," he said. "I'll take a blood sample and test it just to be sure there's no underlying problem, but he looks like he's in great health."

Feather lifted his muzzle to Scott's face and snorted softly.

Amy smiled. Feather really was cute; she could see why Jo adored him so. "If you're not hurting someplace, I guess we better start looking for another reason why you're misbehaving," she said to the gray pony. "Let's find out what's going on in your mind."

"He seems quite highstrung," Scott commented. "Maybe something's scaring him, making him act up."

Amy nodded. Her mom had told her over and over again that the vast majority of behavioral problems were caused by horses either being in pain or being scared. "Ty thought that he looked like the sort of horse that would panic," she said. She studied Feather. "I'll probably get a better idea what's going on in his head when I ride him."

Lou, who had watched the whole examination, frowned. "But what if he rears?"

Amy shrugged. "Better with me than with Jo." And clicking her tongue, she led Feather back to the barn.

Scott followed her, stopping to have a quick look at Jigsaw. The black-and-white pony was resting quietly in his stall, holding his left foreleg out in front of him with the weight on the toe.

"Poor thing," Scott said as he looked at the injured pony. "He works his heart out at a riding school for six years, then this happens, and they send him to a horse sale instead of giving him a nice green pasture."

Amy nodded. "It's not much of a life, is it?" she said. "Being a riding-school pony."

"Depends on the school, I guess," Scott said. "If a pony ends up at the sort of place where Jigsaw was, where the ponies are worked until they break, then no, it can't be a good life."

"But they're not all like that," Lou put in quickly.

"Some are excellent. The horses and ponies are well fed and cared for and work only a reasonable amount —"

She was interrupted by a high-pitched bleeping noise. Scott pulled a pager from his pocket and looked at the message that flashed across it. "Looks like I've got to go," he said. "There's a mare foaling over at Crow's Landing." He kissed Lou quickly. "I'll call you later," he said, and picking up his bag from outside Feather's stall, he set off down the aisle at a jog.

Lou watched him go and then went over to Sugarfoot's stall. "So what have you got planned for this morning?" she asked Amy as she reached over the door and scratched the Shetland affectionately on the neck. Sugarfoot was the only pony that Lou ever showed any real interest in. He'd been half starved when he came to Heartland, and Lou had helped nurse him back to health. Amy knew that the two had developed a true bond.

"First I think I'll work Rosie — see if I can start getting her over her head shyness," Amy said, answering Lou's question. She remembered their conversation the day before about Lou learning to treat the horses. "You could help me, if you want."

Lou shook her head. "I can't. I've got so much stuff to do — things to get ready for this meeting on Monday and invoices to deal with, and I'm in the middle of setting up a new spreadsheet on the computer, and —"

"It's OK, I get the picture," Amy interrupted, thinking that she should have known better than to even bother asking. She started toward the tack room.

"Amy! Hang on!"

Amy stopped, wondering what Lou wanted.

"Maybe I do have time," Lou said, a faint flush of pink coloring her pale cheeks as she left Sugarfoot's stall. "Just for a little bit." Amy stared at her in astonishment. "What, um, do you want me to do?"

"Well, I was going to groom Rosie first," Amy said. "You could give me a hand with that."

"OK."

Rosie was standing at the back of her stall when they arrived with the grooming bucket.

"Good girl," Amy said, clipping a lead rope onto Rosie's halter ring and tying her up.

Lou picked up a rubber curry comb and after a moment's hesitation swept it over the filly's flecked neck and shoulder. "So how are you going to help her?" she asked.

"Well, I'm fairly sure that she's acting up because she's frightened," Amy said, picking up a brush and starting to gently tease out Rosie's sparse chestnut tail. "There's a scar on one of her ears, so I think something happened to her in the past that scared her. What we have to do first is win her trust."

"By joining up with her?" Lou asked, her curry strokes gradually becoming more confident.

Amy nodded. Joining up was a technique that their mom had used a lot. It involved communicating with horses, using body language. "Once I've got her trust, then I can start working on handling her ears and putting a halter on and taking it off."

"She seems really quiet," Lou commented as she began to work on Rosie's hindquarters. "You wouldn't guess she was only three."

"I know," Amy said. Rosie had rested her muzzle on a ledge that ran around the stall wall. Like the day before, her eyes were half closed. Amy felt a flicker of concern. Lou was right, the filly was really very quiet. There wasn't something wrong with her, was there? No, she told herself. Sheri's vet would have spotted it. After all, he'd checked her out only a day or so ago.

"She is OK, isn't she?" Lou said, standing back and frowning at the filly.

"Yeah, I'm sure she is," Amy replied. "Appaloosas were bred to be sensible and obedient."

Still, just to be sure, when they finished grooming, she took Rosie's temperature. It was normal. She shrugged and led Rosie up to the circular ring.

Once in the ring, she unclipped the longline from Rosie's halter. Coiling it neatly, she clicked her tongue and waved the line at Rosie's flank. The filly looked at her in mild surprise but, apart from shifting her hindquarters ninety degrees, didn't move.

"Go on!" Amy said, raising her arms and stepping toward her.

With a slight toss of her head, Rosie turned and trotted away.

Amy walked after her and swung the coiled rope in the direction of Rosie's hindquarters again.

Rosie began to trot around the ring. She tossed her head several times. Keeping her shoulders square to the filly and her eyes on the filly's face, Amy urged her on. With another shake of her head, Rosie broke into a canter. Every time she tried to slow down, Amy stepped toward her, swinging the coiled longline. The aim of joining up with a horse was to get it to choose to be with the human in the middle instead of running away by itself. Only then could she use her body language to show the horse that she was not a threat and to give the horse the chance to ask to be friends.

After four circuits, she moved so that her body was ahead of Rosie's. Raising her arms, she sent the filly around in the other direction.

After another five circuits, Amy got the signal she had been waiting for. The Appaloosa's inside ear flopped down, pointing toward her. She cantered around, her ear seeming to be fixed on Amy. After three more circuits, she began to lower her head. She was trying in her own language to tell Amy that she didn't want to run away from her anymore. Finally, her mouth opened, and slowing to a trot, she started to chew on the air. It was the signal Amy had been waiting for.

Dropping her arms, she immediately turned her body sideways to the horse and lowered her eyes to the ground. I am not a threat, her body language was saying to Rosie. If you want me to be your friend, I will be.

She heard the thud of the Appaloosa's hooves slow from a trot to a walk and from a walk to a halt. Although she was behind Amy, Amy could sense that the horse was looking at her. She waited. One second passed, and then two, and then three, and then she heard a soft snort and the sound of the filly's hooves on the sand.

Amy held her breath. And then she felt what she'd been waiting for — a gentle nuzzling at her shoulder.

Very slowly she turned, and still keeping her eyes averted, she rubbed the filly's nose.

"Good girl," she whispered. Then she turned and walked across the ring. Rosie walked after her, her nose nudging Amy's shoulder. Wherever Amy went, Rosie followed. There was no rope keeping her at Amy's side; she was there because she chose to be. Amy swallowed the happiness bubbling up inside her. Nothing could ever compare to this moment, the moment when a horse overcame its instinct to run away and volunteered its friendship. It was the beginning of a partnership based on trust.

She stopped and stroked Rosie's neck. The filly nuzzled her hand. Her eyes looked at Amy in wonderment. Amy had often seen that expression on the faces of horses she had joined up with — the relief in their eyes, as if they were saying *at last I've found a human who understands.*

"And I do," Amy whispered to the mare. "Or at least I'll do my best to try to."

"Wow!" Lou said from the gate as Amy walked over, with Rosie following her. "It doesn't get any less amazing, no matter how many times you see it."

Amy's eyes glowed. "You should try doing it." Suddenly, she stared at Lou. "Why don't you? You could try it with Rosie right now."

Lou took a quick step back. "No," she said quickly. "I — I wouldn't want to mess things up."

"But you wouldn't," Amy said, longing for Lou to experience the thrill of joining up. "Come on. I'll show you what to do."

But Lou continued to shake her head. "No. I — I'd rather not." She quickly changed the subject. "So what are you going to do with Rosie now?" she asked. "I mean, will she let you touch her ears now that you've joined up with her?"

"Probably not," Amy said, moving one hand experimentally toward the Appaloosa's ears. As she expected, the filly jerked her head away.

"Oh," Lou said, looking disappointed.

"Joining up isn't a miracle cure for all problems," Amy explained. "It's more of a step in the right direction. By having joined up with her, I made it easier to help her overcome her fear, because she knows I'm basically not a threat. But it's too deep-seated a fear to be overcome just by joining up."

"So what do you do now?" Lou asked, looking fascinated.

"Now I give her a choice. She can accept my touch, or she can move away from me, but if she moves away she has to stay away."

"I don't get it," Lou said.

"Watch," Amy said, leading Rosie back into the center of the ring. Once again she put her hand up by Rosie's ear. The second the filly shied away, Amy immediately raised her arms in the air and sent the horse cantering back around the pen. After three circuits, Rosie was giving signals that she wanted to be allowed into the center again. As her mouth started to open and close, Amy turned her shoulders inward and, through her body language, invited the filly to approach.

Once Rosie had followed her around the ring a few times, Amy started to feel all over her body. As Amy's hands reached her ears, Rosie shied back, and once again Amy raised her arms and sent her cantering round the outside.

"Do you see?" she called to Lou. "I'm giving her a

choice. She can either choose to stay beside me and have her ears handled or she can choose to go away — it's up to her. But if she chooses to go away, then she has to stay away until I'm ready to let her come in and be near me again. I'm not forcing her to have her ears touched. I'm letting her make the choice."

Three times Rosie came in and then shied away when Amy tried to handle her ears. But on the fourth time she actually stood still and let Amy stroke the base of her ears.

"Good girl." Amy praised Rosie, rewarding the filly's good behavior by immediately moving her hand away. She rubbed Rosie's neck and then tried again. Rosie stiffened, but she stood still as Amy stroked around both ears.

"That's great," Lou said. "It's a huge improvement."

"The best part is that it's all done without force," Amy said with delight. She patted Rosie's neck. "OK, girl. That'll do for today."

"So how long do you think it will take to cure her completely?" Lou asked as they led Rosie back down to her stall.

"Hopefully not that long," Amy said. "She might be OK in a week or so, though it depends on the horse."

"Are you going to try to cure her head tossing as well?" Lou said as Rosie lifted her muzzle and circled it swiftly through the air. "I noticed she was doing it quite a bit out in the ring."

Amy frowned. She'd been so focused on the joining

up that she hadn't really noticed Rosie shaking her head, but now that Lou mentioned it, she remembered the filly had been doing it a lot.

"She's not going to make much of a pleasure horse if she does it when she's being ridden," Lou commented.

Amy nodded. "You're right. I'd better give Sheri a call and talk to her about it. See if she's noticed."

As Lou helped her give Rosie a quick brush to remove the traces of sweat and dust, Amy felt a glow of contentment. *If only things could always be like this,* she thought as she watched her sister sweeping a body brush over Rosie's spotted flanks. It felt good sharing her thoughts on Rosie with Lou. So often it seemed as if they didn't have that much in common. Lou was always busy in the office, while Amy was out in the yard. They hardly ever just chatted or hung out together. And for once, Amy noticed, looking at her sister's face, Lou actually looked relaxed.

After Rosie had been put in her stall, Lou helped Amy groom two of the other boarders, Maddison, a show horse that hated being trailered, and Sovereign, a young Morgan that had come to Heartland to have his fear of traffic cured.

"You know," Lou said as they finished Maddison, "I've been thinking. I really enjoyed watching you with Rosie today. Maybe I really should get more involved with treating the horses."

Amy was surprised but pleased. "That would be great," she said.

Lou's eyes shone with a sudden enthusiasm. "It would, wouldn't it? I could specialize in some sort of treatment, one that you and Ty don't use that much, homeopathy or something like that. Or there's this form of treatment using magnets that I read about in a magazine. Maybe I could become Heartland's magnotherapy expert."

Amy felt a prickling of unease. She'd been imagining Lou helping her and Ty. She wasn't sure she wanted her sister to become an expert.

"What do you think?" Lou demanded.

Amy hesitated. "Well, maybe," she said doubtfully. "But what about learning the treatments we already use first? You could help Ty and me just to get started, like Ben's doing." She saw Lou's face tighten.

"You don't think it's a good idea," Lou said flatly.

"No, it's great. It's just kind of sudden," Amy said, trying to be tactful. "Maybe you could pick something to specialize in after you have more experience."

Lou gave a measured nod. "It was a dumb idea," she said.

"It wasn't," Amy protested. "I'd like you to help more."

But Lou didn't seem to be listening. She put down the brush she was holding and glanced at her watch. "I'd better go in," she said. "I've got lots to do." She forced a smile. "It was fun, but I'm busy enough as it is without taking on more responsibilities."

"So you're not going to start learning about treating the horses?" Amy asked as Lou headed for the stall door.

"I think I'll leave that to you and Ty for now," Lou said as she turned and walked away.

Amy watched her go. She felt bad. She'd like to have Lou to help more, just not to take over. But that was her sister's nature. Lou couldn't ever get just a little involved in anything. If she decided something was worth doing, then she put every ounce of herself into it.

Amy sighed and carried the grooming box around to Jake's stall. She had just started grooming him when Jo came up the driveway.

"Hi," she said, jogging over. "I've come to see Feather. How is he? Have you done anything with him? Is he OK?" The words tumbled out in her eagerness. Before Amy could answer, Jo noticed Jake. "Wow!" she gasped, looking at the enormous Clydesdale. "He's big! What's his name?"

"Jake," Amy replied, trying to figure out which order to answer the questions in. "Feather's OK. The vet checked him over earlier and said he seems just fine, but I haven't started working with him yet."

"So where is he?" Jo asked, looking around eagerly.

"In the back barn," Amy said, throwing her grooming brush into a bucket. "Come on, I'll show you."

"I would just love to live in a place like this," Jo said as they walked up the yard. "You are so totally lucky."

Amy smiled. "I know. So how's your mom?"

"A nightmare," Jo said, rolling her eyes. "The way she keeps going on you'd think Feather was about to win the most dangerous horse of the year award."

"You did well to stay on him when he reared like that," Amy said. "How long have you been riding?"

"Since I was seven," Jo replied. "I wanted to start before that, but Mom wouldn't let me. She wasn't even that thrilled about me starting then, but Dad persuaded her."

"So why doesn't your mom like horses?" Amy asked.

"She's scared of them," Jo sighed. "When she was four, my grandma had a riding accident. She ended up in a wheelchair, and the horse she was riding had to be put down. Mom's been terrified of horses ever since. I think if she had her way I'd have a hobby like" — she wrinkled her nose in disgust — "embroidery or stamp collecting. She's been even worse about me riding since she and Dad split up last year. She just seems to want to protect me all the time." For a moment her face looked downcast. "I don't like Mom getting upset, but I can't not ride. I love horses, and I love Feather most of all." They had entered the back barn. Suddenly, Jo saw Feather's gray head looking over his door. "Feather!" she cried happily.

The pretty gray pony pricked his ears and whinnied. Jo raced down the aisle and flung her arms around his neck. "Hey, boy. How are you?" she said, kissing him several times on his soft nose. He nuzzled her.

"I think he's happy to see you," Amy said, smiling.

"Not as much as I am to see him," Jo said. She hugged him hard. "I don't care what Mom says, I'm never, ever going to let him go."

Amy felt a chill of apprehension run through her as she heard Jo's words. She hoped that she was going to be able to cure Feather. But what if she couldn't? What would Jo do then?

Chapter Four

"So how was Feather when you rode him?" Soraya Martin asked as she and Amy sorted out their books at their lockers the next morning. For most of the bus ride to Jefferson High, Amy had been so busy finishing her homework assignments that she hadn't had time to talk. It was only now that she'd finally started to fill her best friend in on the events of the weekend.

"Great," she replied, thinking back to her ride on Feather the day before.

"He didn't try to rear?" Soraya said, pulling her black shoulder-length curls off her face with a hair clip.

"Not a hint," Amy said. Feather had obviously been well schooled and was very responsive. In fact, far from being a problem, he'd been a joy to ride.

Soraya looked puzzled. "Why was he so bad on Saturday then?"

"I don't know," Amy admitted. "It's weird. Jo watched
me ride him yesterday and said that's how he normally
is. He's apparently only reared a couple of times. But un-
fortunately, her mom was watching each time, so now
Mrs. Newhart's convinced he's too dangerous to ride."
She shut her locker and leaned back against it, frowning. "There's got to be something that's triggering his
bad behavior, but until he starts acting up, I'm not going
to be able to find out what it is."

"Sounds like you're just going to have to wait," Soraya
said.

Amy nodded. "The trouble is, Mrs. Newhart's only
going to give me until the end of the month. If he's not
better by then she's going to make Jo sell him."

"Poor Jo," Soraya said as they started along the busy
hall toward their homeroom.

"I just hope we can cure him in time," Amy said.

"I'm sure you will," Soraya said reassuringly.

"Give me a break. Heartland? Cure a horse?" a familiar
voice drawled from behind them. "That would be a first."

Amy swung around. Ashley Grant was standing by
the lockers, her arms crossed, her perfectly plucked eyebrows raised in a disbelieving line. Beside her stood her
two friends, Jade and Brittany. They were grinning.

"Come on, Amy," Soraya said. "She isn't worth it."

But Amy ignored her. "We've helped more horses at Heartland than you ever will at Green Briar," she snapped, glaring at Ashley.

Green Briar was the hunter barn that was run by Ashley's mom and dad. Using strong discipline and force, her mom, Val Grant, specialized in producing push-button horses and ponies that could be relied on to rack up the ribbons. She also had a sideline in dealing with horses with behavioral problems. Her methods were, however, very different from those used at Heartland.

Ashley tossed her platinum blond hair over her shoulder and tut-tutted. "Exaggerating again, Amy. Math never has been your strong point, has it? We have three twenty-stall barns, four schooling rings, one covered arena, and a cross-country course. What do you have at Heartland? Let me see," she pretended to think. "Well, there's a single barn, a falling-down stable block, and two scrappy little rings. Yeah, I think we might just have dealt with a few more horses than you."

Despite the blood that was beating through her brain, Amy stared at her coolly. "I didn't say dealt with, Ashley, I said helped. You and your family don't know the meaning of the word." She saw Ashley stiffen slightly as her words hit home, and Amy turned to go.

"Meaning you do?" Ashley said, recovering herself

quickly. "Oh, yeah, Amy, I'm sorry, I forgot. You're a horse whisperer, aren't you?"

Jade and Brittany giggled.

Amy glared at her. She didn't like it when people assumed that she just whispered to horses and then they did what she said. She didn't do anything of the sort. She listened to what horses tried to communicate to her. "I am not a horse whisperer," she said hotly. "I don't — *ouch*!" Soraya elbowed her in the ribs. Amy turned on her friend. "What are you —?"

Before she could finish, she realized why Soraya had nudged her. Matt Trewin, one of their best friends and, much to Amy's disgust, Ashley's current boyfriend, was approaching. "What's happening?" he inquired as he looked from Amy to Ashley.

"Nothing," Amy said quickly. When Matt had first started dating Ashley, she had almost lost his friendship by telling him what she thought of his choice of girl-friend. Since then, she'd been trying to hold in her dislike of Ashley—at least when he was around.

The snideness vanished from Ashley's face. "We were just talking," Ashley said, going over and taking Matt's arm possessively. "In fact, I was just about to tell Amy some good news."

Amy caught a smug look in Ashley's eyes that suggested that whatever the news was, Amy certainly wasn't going to class it as good. "What?" she said suspiciously.

"Oh, just that we might be seeing much more of each other in the future," Ashley said. "Daddy's heard there's some land coming up for sale right beside Heartland, and he's going to put in an offer. He thinks it would be perfect for us to extend our facilities. He wants to build an eventing course and training center."

"What?" Amy stared at her. "Which land?"

"The Youngs' land," Ashley told her.

"I didn't know that was for sale!" Amy exclaimed, thinking of the fields to the east of Heartland.

"Well, why would they tell you?" Ashley said. "I mean, it's not like Heartland could afford to buy it, is it?" Her green eyes danced at Amy, as if daring her to have an outburst in front of Matt. "Won't it be nice?" she cooed in a voice that dripped with saccharine sweetness. "We'll be neighbors, Amy."

Amy saw Matt glance swiftly at Ashley. He wasn't stupid, and although she knew he desperately wanted to believe that she and Ashley had called a truce, she was sure that he knew exactly how things were between them.

"Lost your voice, Amy?" Ashley said, the triumphant taunt in her voice only barely concealed.

Amy bit back the sharp words that sprang to her tongue. She wasn't going to be goaded into a fight in front of Matt. "No, Ashley," she said coolly. "It's just that I like to think before I speak — something you rarely do."

And with that, she took hold of Soraya's arm and walked away.

"Wow!" Soraya said as soon as they had turned the corner. "I thought you were going to freak when she talked about that farm, but you were awesome. You kept so cool!"

Amy stopped at the watercooler and took a deep breath. "But do you think she's telling the truth? Do you think the Youngs could be selling their land?"

"I don't know." Soraya looked doubtful. "You know what Ashley's like — full of a lot of hot air most of the time. I'm sure you would have heard about it if there was anything to it."

"You're right," Amy said. "Ashley's probably just trying to get to me. I won't think about it anymore. Now come on, we've got a math class to get to!"

Ty was grooming Dancer when Amy got back from school that afternoon.

"Hey, there," he called. His tousled hair had fallen over his forehead, and as Amy went over to him, she had to fight a sudden urge to straighten it.

"So how was school?" Ty asked her.

"Same as always." Amy suddenly remembered her news. "Though you'll never guess what Ashley told me —"

She relayed what Ashley had said.

"Green Briar next door!" Ty said. "No way! Anyway, I'm sure we'd have heard about it if the Youngs really were selling their farm."

"I know," Amy agreed. "That's what Soraya said. Even so, it's too deeply scary to even think about." She shuddered. "Tell me something good. How have the horses been today?"

"All fine," Ty replied. And he started giving her a rundown on what he and Ben had been doing. "I haven't done anything with Rosie and Feather," he finished. "I thought it would be better to wait till you got home."

Amy nodded. "I'll work them in the ring," she said. "Then maybe we could take Moochie and Sundance out for a ride."

"Sure," Ty agreed with a smile.

❧

An hour and a half later, Amy and Ty rode out of Heartland.

"We had a phone call this morning from a woman asking if we had any horses that needed rehoming," Ty said as they headed onto the trail that led up Teak's Hill, the wooded mountain behind Heartland. "She wants a horse for pleasure riding." He patted Moochie's neck. "I thought Moochie might suit her. She wants to know when she can come and visit."

"Tell her she can come and see him this —" Amy broke off. She'd been about to say this weekend, but suddenly she remembered about her father's visit. "A week from Sunday," she corrected herself and fell into silence, her fingers playing in Sundance's dark mane.

She'd been so busy all day that she'd almost forgotten about her father's visit, but there was no getting away from it. Every second that passed was bringing the weekend closer.

"Thinking about your dad?" Ty asked, riding Moochie up alongside her.

Amy looked at Sundance's golden ears. "Why does he have to come? We're happy without him. Mom never wanted him here. When he wrote to her, she didn't reply. She didn't want him back in our lives."

"I know," Ty said. "But Lou does."

Amy nodded slowly. He was right. She was doing this for Lou. That's what she had to remember.

🐍

When they got back from their ride, Lou was just getting out of her car. She'd been at her meeting in town, and judging from the excited expression on her face, Amy guessed that it had gone well.

"So are you going to tell me about it now?" she asked Lou.

"You bet I am," Lou grinned. "Amy Fleming, we just might be about to buy some more land! The Youngs are selling their farm. Come on, I'll tell you all about it over supper!"

Chapter Five

"A riding school!" Amy exclaimed. She stared at her sister in utter astonishment — and growing horror. "Your plan is to have a riding school?"

Lou nodded, her eyes glowing as she looked from Grandpa to Amy. "Yeah, isn't it a brilliant idea? I can't believe Mom never thought of it. It will bring in money to help pay for the rehabilitation side of things, and we can even use some of the horses and ponies we rescue. It was when Jigsaw came that I had the idea," she said. "It would be so easy. We could get more ponies like him, make them better, and then use them to give riding lessons."

Amy shook her head. "It won't work. The horses we rescue are either traumatized or physically damaged. A pony like Jigsaw is never going to be fit for anything more than light work."

Lou bit her lip for a moment. "Well, we could look for horses and ponies that aren't as badly injured as Jigsaw," she said. "There are sales all the time. We could find horses that just need some better care and conditioning. Anyway, that's why I had this meeting today. I heard the Youngs were selling some of the land that adjoins Heartland, so I arranged a meeting with the bank, and they've agreed to give us a loan — well, in principle anyway. We'll have money to buy the land, find some horses, and hire a trainer and another stable hand. Of course, Grandpa, I need to let you know that we'd be using Heartland as collateral. The bank insisted on it. They also want us to prepare a formal business plan before they'll approve the loan."

"You mean you went to the bank to secure a loan using Heartland, and you didn't even ask me?" Jack's words cut through the air.

Lou stared at him, color creeping into her cheeks. "Well, they brought up the issue of collateral and I didn't think you'd mind. You've always said that you'd leave the business side of Heartland up to me, Grandpa."

"I didn't mean deciding something like this," Jack stated firmly. "Whether we should have a brochure and what sort of fund-raising event we should have is one thing, but taking out a loan on the farm is quite another. Heartland belongs to me. It's my land."

Lou rubbed her forehead as she looked down at her plate. "I'm sorry, Grandpa. I — I just wanted to see if it was possible. I was only trying to do what I thought was best."

Grandpa's voice softened. "I know you were, honey," he said, reaching out to cover her hand with his own. "And I'm not saying no to your idea. I'm just saying that we need to talk about it before we go steaming ahead."

"We sure do!" Amy exclaimed, suddenly recovering from the shock she was feeling and realizing she had to speak out. "I don't want a riding school here."

"Why not?"

The surprise in Lou's eyes seemed genuine, and although Amy felt like shouting at her, she forced herself to keep calm. "It will get in the way of the work we do."

"But it doesn't have to," Lou protested. "In fact, it could complement it. You could teach the riding school students about alternative therapies, and they could help out in the main yard during vacations and on weekends."

For a moment, Amy considered it. Maybe they could have a riding school where the ponies were happy and the students learned to listen to horses. Yes, it would be great to spread the ideals of Heartland to young riders. But it would also mean Heartland would get bigger. They'd have to have more staff, and there'd be people coming and going all the time. Did she really want Heartland to be like that? "I — I'm not sure, Lou," she said.

"Look," Lou said. "Let me at least put together the business plan. It will take me most of the week, and that will give you both some more time to think about it. If we decide that we don't want go ahead, then we just won't take it any further."

"OK," Jack said slowly. He glanced across at Amy. "Is that all right with you? We can think about it some more and then decide as a family."

Amy nodded. "Look, there's something else you should know." She frowned. "We might not get this extra land anyway, Lou. Ashley Grant told me at school today that her dad wants to buy it to extend Green Briar."

Lou looked worried. "You're kidding! We'd better get moving then," Lou said. "I might go and speak to the Youngs and let them know we're interested. Maybe we can come to some arrangement before it goes on the open market." Her eyes shone as she looked around at them. "I know this can work — I just know it!"

"Have you told Ty about Lou's plan?" Soraya asked the next day as they had lunch in the cafeteria.

Amy nodded. "I called him last night."

"What did he say?"

Amy moved closer so she could speak over the noise of the other students. "He wasn't thrilled, but he says that if it happens, it happens." She sighed. "I know Lou's good at business, but sometimes she gets so hung up on bringing in money she doesn't think about whether it's a good idea for other reasons."

Soraya nodded. "It must be tough for her. I guess she's still trying to prove herself."

"What do you mean?" Amy asked, surprised.

Soraya tucked a stray curl behind her left ear and looked thoughtful. "Well, she had that big job in New York before she came back to Heartland. I can see why she isn't content to just do the accounts and things. I guess she wants to make her mark — to be as successful at Heartland as she was in the city. Especially with your dad coming. She's going to want him to feel proud of her, isn't she?"

Amy stared at her friend. "I hadn't thought about it like that before, but you could be right." She grimaced. "I just wish it didn't mean her coming up with ideas like this. I can't say no because I know it means so much to her, but I don't want to say yes."

"Well, maybe the Grants will get the land," Soraya said.

"Thanks a lot," said Amy, getting up to dump her trash. "That's not a solution!"

"So how are you feeling about your dad coming?" Soraya asked as they walked out onto the school grounds.

"I don't want to think about it," Amy said with a shudder. She changed the subject quickly. "Ben asked about you last night. He wanted to know where you'd been."

"Did you tell him I was rehearsing for this play?" Soraya said quickly. She was playing the lead in the school play and hadn't been to Heartland as much as usual lately.

"No, I told him you were on the moon." Amy grinned. "What do you think I said?" She shook her head. "You know, I wish you two would just get it together."

"That would be fine by me," Soraya said. "Anyhow, you should talk. Look at you and Ty. I don't know why you don't just admit you like each other and start dating for real."

"I don't want to," Amy protested. "You know what people are like when they date. I don't want to spend all my time talking and thinking about him and worrying about our relationship."

At that moment, Soraya saw Matt, who was standing with Ashley by the entrance to the school. She shot Amy a sideways look. "I wonder how Matt would take the news that you and Ty are dating. After all, didn't you tell him that you wouldn't go out with him because you didn't want to risk your friendship?"

"Yeah," Amy said uncomfortably. "But Ty and I aren't dating. Besides, Matt doesn't like me anymore. He's got Ashley now."

"Like that's going to last!" Soraya said. "Did you hear her bossing him around this morning after biology? He's not going to put up with that sort of treatment for long."

Amy raised her eyebrows. "He seems to be coping pretty well right at the moment," she said as Matt put his arm around Ashley's shoulders.

✇

After school, Amy changed clothes and then worked Rosie in the ring. Although it was only three days since she had first joined up with her, the filly was already much better at having her ears handled and a halter put on. As usual, Amy started the session with a join up, and then, once Rosie was willingly following her around, she started to stroke the filly's head. Working her fingers in small circles, she reached Rosie's ears. Rosie stood still. Trying hard to keep her breathing relaxed, Amy un-buckled the halter. Rosie started slightly as it slid off her nose.

"Easy now," Amy said soothingly.

She brought the halter up to the mare's nose again. But the movement was too much for Rosie. With a snort she shied away. "OK then, off you go," Amy said, raising her arms and sending the mare trotting around the ring. As she kept the mare going, she found herself wondering what her father would say when he saw how they worked with the horses at Heartland. Her mom had gotten into using alternative therapies through trying to help Pegasus, Amy's dad's great show jumper. Conventional medicine had helped him only so much, then Marion had begun to search for other solutions. It was the knowledge she had gained from treating Pegasus that led to helping other damaged horses at Heartland.

Amy wondered again about her father. *He's probably into traditional training techniques,* she thought bitterly. *He won't understand our work at all.*

It took only a few circuits before Rosie started to let Amy know that she wanted to be allowed to come in close again. This time when Amy tried with the halter, the filly stood still and let her slip it on and buckle it up.

"Good girl," Amy praised, delighted.

"She's really coming along," Ty's voice said behind her.

Amy turned. "She is, isn't she?"

"Still tossing her head though," Ty said as Rosie circled her head in the air.

"I know," Amy said. She'd spoken to Sheri about it, but Sheri had said she'd never noticed it.

"Hi!" They turned to see Jo-Ann jumping out of her brother's car and coming toward them.

"Hey," Amy called.

"Have you ridden Feather today?" When Amy shook her head Jo said, "Could I groom him then?"

"Sure," Amy replied.

Jo ran back down the yard and Ty smiled. "She's nice."

"Yeah, really nice," Amy said. "And she's picking up on T-touch well. She's been doing it on him once or twice a day and massaging in the violet leaf oil like I showed her. He seems to love all the fuss."

"But we still don't have any idea what the problem is," Ty said.

"No," Amy said. "Until he misbehaves there's not much I can do," she said. "Maybe tonight will be the night."

But Feather was as good as ever. He walked, trotted, and cantered in serpentines and figure eights. Amy even popped him over a small jump, and there wasn't a hint of him acting up.

"It's like he can read my mind," Amy said, stopping by the fence to talk to Jo. "I only have to think about turning or changing pace and he does it." She patted his neck. "You're one cool pony, Feather." He snorted and nodded his head.

Jo laughed. "See, he understands every word you say." She looked at him longingly. "Can't I ride him?" she begged. "Mom would never know."

Amy reluctantly shook her head. "Sorry, but you know what your mom said. Not until we're really sure that he's safe."

"But it's so unfair!" Jo exclaimed. She caught Amy's look and piped down a little. "I just want to ride him so much," she said and sighed.

❧

For the rest of the week, Feather continued to behave perfectly. By Friday, Amy was at her wit's end. "We've only got three weeks left with him, Ty, and we still don't know why he reared with Jo," she said, feeling frustrated as they filled the evening hay nets. "And with my" — she almost muttered the word — "father here this weekend, I probably won't have that much time to work with him."

"Maybe we should let Jo ride him," Ty said. "See what he does."

Amy pulled the drawstring on the hay net tight. "OK, maybe I'll give Mrs. Newhart a call tonight and see what she says."

"Didn't Jo say she and her mom were out of town for the weekend?" Ty said.

"Oh, yeah," Amy said, remembering that Jo had told her she wouldn't be at Heartland again till Monday. "I'll call Monday."

Lou came into the feed room. She had a notebook and pencil. "I've got a few questions to ask you," she said.

Amy groaned inwardly. Ever since Lou had started

preparing the business plan for the bank, she was constantly asking questions about the riding school.

"Now, how many hours do you think a pony could work each day?" she said. "And how much feed would each pony need?"

The questions went on until Amy wanted to scream. The more Lou talked about a riding school, the less Amy wanted one at Heartland.

But what can I say? she thought as she walked to the house. She knew she needed to work with Lou as much as possible.

Before she went inside, she took a last look around. Ty and Ben, well aware of her anxiety at meeting her father the next morning, had tidied the whole place up. Amy felt really touched by their efforts.

"It's not as if I care what he thinks," she muttered as she pulled off her boots.

Going into the house, she met Grandpa. He was just about to go out for dinner with Ken and Marie, friends of his, and his usual jeans and sweater had been replaced by a duck-egg blue open-necked shirt and chinos. "I'd better get moving," he said, picking up his car keys. "Lou's gone to Scott's for the evening. Are you sure you'll be OK on your own?"

"I'll be just fine," Amy said, flopping down in one of the armchairs. "You have a good time."

"Thanks," Jack said. "There's some ham in the refrigerator for supper." He came over and kissed the top of her head. "I'll see you later."

Jack went out through the door, and a few minutes later Amy heard him drive away.

The room suddenly seemed very quiet. She leaned her head against the back of the armchair. She hardly ever spent evenings on her own. What should she do?

Eat first, she decided, as her stomach growled loudly into the silence.

Getting to her feet, she made a couple of bagels with cream cheese and some of the ham that Grandpa had baked. Putting them on a plate, she went upstairs. Maybe she should get started on her weekend homework.

But when she sat down at the desk and opened her history book, the words she was reading refused to go into her head. She kept thinking about the next day and meeting her father. After she had read and reread the first paragraph five times, she finally gave up.

Closing her history book, she picked up a photograph of her mom that she kept on her desk. It showed her standing by Pegasus's pasture gate. The big gray Thoroughbred was nuzzling her mom's fair hair, and Marion was laughing. The picture had been taken just a few weeks before the accident.

"Oh, Mom," Amy whispered, touching the picture with her lips. "What would you say if you knew Daddy was coming here tomorrow? What would you tell me to do?"

She shut her eyes. But there was no answer. She was on her own.

Chapter Six

"You're going to spend the weekend with Ken and Marie!" Amy exclaimed, staring at Grandpa the next morning.

Jack nodded. "You know they've just moved, and it sounds like they could really use a hand getting their yard in order," he said. "I've offered to put in some runs for their dogs. It'll be easier all around if I stay there overnight."

"But what about Daddy?" Lou said. "You won't see him at all if you're away all weekend."

"I know, but I've thought about it, and I figure it's better this way," Jack said. "You two need some space with your father on your own." Lou opened her mouth. "I've made up my mind, Lou," Jack said before she could argue. "And I'm not going to change it."

Lou looked at his stubborn face. "All right," she said reluctantly. "If you think it's for the best."

Grandpa nodded. "Believe me, it is."

As he left the kitchen to get his things together, Lou picked up a sponge from the sink and started to wipe off the kitchen table. "This place needs cleaning before Daddy gets here."

Snagging her jacket off the back of the door, Amy went outside. Maybe keeping busy would help keep her butterflies at bay, too.

At quarter to ten, Amy left Ty and Ben to finish the remaining stalls and reluctantly went inside to shower. When she came downstairs, Lou was hovering by the kitchen window. Every surface was spotless, and a vase of freshly cut flowers was on the table.

Not knowing what to do with herself, Amy sat down at the table. It was impossible to sit still. Every nerve in her body felt stretched to the breaking point. She bounced one foot up and down on the floor, and when that didn't help she started to drum her fingers on the tabletop.

"Amy!" Lou snapped, swinging around. "Stop that!"

Amy looked up with a start.

Lou's face softened. "I'm sorry," she sighed. "I guess I'm just a bit tense."

"It's OK," Amy said. "Me, too." She got to her feet and

walked restlessly around the kitchen. The butterflies were getting worse now. She could feel a wave of panic swelling inside her.

I don't want to be here, she thought. *I don't want him to come here.*

But it was too late.

"Here he is!" Lou said, her voice rising in excitement as she flew to the door.

Amy followed, her heart pounding. A silver Volvo had just parked outside the house, and a tall man was getting out.

"Daddy!" Lou gasped.

For a moment, Amy thought that Lou was going to run to fling her arms around his neck. But at the last minute something seemed to stop her. "Hello," she said, coming to a halt in front of the car.

"Hello, Lou," Tim Fleming said, his English accent sounding clipped and precise. He walked toward Lou and shook his head wonderingly. "It's lovely to see you!" he said, taking her hands. "You've certainly grown." His eyes lifted, and he looked at Amy. "Amy?"

Wishing she were somewhere — anywhere — else, Amy nodded. Her father came over to her, his gaze riveted on her face. He reached out for her hands, too, but Amy kept them firmly in her pockets.

Tim's hands dropped, but his eyes continued searching her face. "I can't believe it's you," he said.

Maybe that's because you haven't seen me in twelve years, Amy thought, but she kept the sharp answer to herself. She shrugged. "Well, it is."

He had changed so much from the photos. His tanned skin was carved into deep grooves and lines, and his gray eyes looked shadowed.

"Should we go inside and have some coffee?" Lou said.

Tim nodded. "That would be nice."

Amy followed them into the kitchen. While Lou began opening cupboards, Tim looked at the photographs on the kitchen wall. "I remember that," he said, putting his finger on one of the framed photographs of Marion jumping at Hickstead, an international show in England.

Don't touch it! Amy wanted to snap.

"Your mother was a brilliant show jumper," Tim said, turning to her.

"I know," Amy said coldly. "Grandpa told me."

"Where is Jack?" Tim asked.

"He's away for the weekend," Lou said quickly. "He — he had to help some friends out."

Tim sighed. "And wanted to avoid seeing me."

Lou fumbled with the coffeemaker. "It wasn't like that," she began. "These friends of his, they've just moved, and —"

"It's OK, Lou," Tim interrupted. "You don't have to make excuses. I can understand why Jack might not want to see me."

"Like you can blame him," Amy said, the words darting out before she could stop them.

"Amy!" Lou said.

Amy looked mutinously at the floor, but not before she had caught Tim glancing quickly in her direction.

There was an awkward silence for a moment, and then Tim cleared his throat. "Well, Lou, do you want a hand with that coffee?"

"It's OK," Lou said. "It's nearly ready."

Amy could hear the irritation in Lou's voice and knew that it was because of her. Mentally, she kicked herself. She hadn't meant to make Lou mad. Why couldn't she have kept her thoughts to herself? "I'll get the mugs, Lou," she offered, eager to make up.

Lou's frosty expression thawed slightly. "Thanks."

Amy put out the mugs and the milk, and Lou poured the coffee. "Light with one sugar?" she said, smiling at Tim. "I remember how you like it."

"Actually, Lou," Tim said, putting his hand over the cup before she could add milk, "just black would be fine."

"Oh, OK," Lou said, looking slightly taken aback.

For a moment no one spoke, and then Lou broke the silence.

"You said on the phone at Christmas that your wife had just had a baby," she said to Tim. "Did — did you bring any pictures with you?"

"I did," Tim said, a sudden smile turning up the corners of his mouth. He pulled his wallet out of his pocket. "Here she is," he said proudly as he handed them a photo of a baby with a shock of light brown hair. "We named her Lily."

"She's so sweet," Lou said quietly.

Tim looked at Amy. "She's just like you when you were that age."

Amy stared at the baby in the photograph. It was just too weird to think that she and the baby were half sisters. She placed the photograph on the kitchen table without saying a word.

"And this is one of the two of you when you were little," Tim said, taking out another photograph and showing it to them. It was a picture of them playing on a beach together when Amy was about three. Amy had seen a similar one in her mom's photo album. "I carry it everywhere with me," Tim said quietly.

The silence seemed to swell as Amy and Lou looked down at the old photograph. Finally, Tim cleared his throat. "So, er, Amy," he said, picking up the photographs and putting them away, "how are you doing in school?"

"Fine," Amy muttered, her thoughts whirling.

Tim waited as if expecting her to say more. When she didn't, he nodded. "That's good." He cleared his throat again. "And Lou. You said in your letter that you used to work in Manhattan."

"Yes. I was with Citibank," Lou said, seeming to come

out of a trance. "I did an MBA when I finished at Oxford, and then I got a job over here. I'd been working for Citibank for just over a year when" — she hesitated — "when Mom had her accident."

Tim nodded. "Then you gave it all up to come back here."

"That's right," Lou said. "I wasn't sure I'd done the best thing for a while. I loved the thrill and pace of working in New York." As she spoke her eyes glowed.

"I see," Tim said, but Amy thought his tone suggested he was agreeing more out of politeness than because he really understood how Lou felt.

"Anyway," Lou continued, "now I run the business side of things here. I'm in the middle of developing a business plan to start a riding school — if we can get a loan approved to buy the land we need."

"We're not actually committed to it yet," Amy said quickly. She felt Tim glance at her, but she kept her eyes on Lou. "Grandpa hasn't said yes yet."

"But he will," Lou said, shooting her a look that said quite clearly that Amy shouldn't argue. She smiled at Tim. "It's a big job, you know."

"It certainly is." Tim frowned slightly. "From what I've heard, I thought your main concern here was rescuing horses."

"It is, but to run a sanctuary like this you need to

bring in a lot of money," Lou said. "A riding school would be the perfect answer."

"I wouldn't have thought a riding school would bring in that much money," Tim said thoughtfully. "They're not known for being hugely profitable. Are you sure it's a wise decision?"

"Yes," Lou said sharply.

"Lou's right." Despite her doubts about the riding school, Amy found herself leaping to her sister's defense when she saw a hurt look flickering through Lou's eyes. "Of course she's thought it all through and made sure it would be a success. She wouldn't have suggested it otherwise."

Lou looked at her in surprise but then smiled gratefully.

Tim nodded uncomfortably and didn't say anything more.

The silence stretched out. Unable to bear the tension in the room, Amy got to her feet. "I'm going to check on the horses. Would you like to see the yard?" she offered.

Tim stood up quickly. "That would be great."

As Amy led the way to the yard, she thought about this meeting with their dad. It wasn't going like she'd imagined it at all. She'd thought that he and Lou would be talking nonstop about the good old days. But nothing could be further from the truth. There was only one word to describe the atmosphere and that was awkward.

"How many horses do you have here?" Tim asked her as the three of them walked to the front stable block.

"Eighteen," Amy replied. "Eight rescue, eight boarders, my pony, Sundance, and Red over there," she nodded to the big chestnut that was looking out over his stall door. "He belongs to Ben, one of our stable hands."

"Hello, boy," Tim said, going over and offering the back of his hand to the chestnut gelding. Red bent his head and snuffled at him. Tim rubbed his nose. "You're a fine-looking horse, aren't you?"

Although Amy didn't want to be overfriendly to her dad, she couldn't help agreeing. "He is, isn't he? He's a Thoroughbred-Hanoverian cross. Ben competes him in High Prelim, but the way he jumps he's going to upgrade really quickly."

Just then Ben came out of the tack room. Seeing that they were by Red's stall, he came over.

Lou introduced him to their father.

"Pleased to meet you, sir," Ben said, holding out his hand.

"Likewise," Tim said. "I was just admiring Red. He's certainly a looker. Amy says you jump him?"

"Yes," Ben said, his face lighting up at Tim's praise for Red. "I've had him since he was three. I backed him myself, and I've been training him ever since then."

"Good for you," Tim said, stroking Red's neck. "Maybe I could watch you ride him later on."

"Sure!" Ben said, looking delighted. "I'll put some more fences up at lunchtime, so there will be a full course."

Amy looked at Ben in surprise. Why was he looking so thrilled? Then it dawned on her. To Ben, her father was Tim Fleming, the former Olympic show jumper who had won championships all over the world. Of course Ben was delighted that he wanted to see Red jump.

Just then Ty came down the yard to say hello.

"How long have you been working here, Ty?" Tim said as they shook hands.

"Three years," Ty replied.

"I'd love to hear about the work you do," Tim went on. He looked at Amy. "I've been investigating the use of natural remedies over the past few years. It would be great to pick your brains and learn some more."

Amy studied her father suspiciously, but he looked as if he meant what he said.

"Sure," Ty said. "I could talk about our techniques all day if you'd let me."

Tim smiled. "Sounds great." He looked around. "Do I get to meet the rest of the horses now?"

As Amy led the way around the rest of the yard, she felt herself relaxing slightly. Introducing her father to the horses was a hundred times better than sitting in the kitchen. For a start, he seemed to relax more around the horses, and she had to admit he was very good with them. He didn't force his presence on them but waited until they came to say hello to him. Then, stroking them gently, he murmured soft words to them. Without exception, they responded.

Watching as even Rosie bent her head and allowed him to scratch her forehead, Amy felt surprised. For some reason, she hadn't expected him to be so good with horses. She should have known that he would be — after all, he had spent his life with them. But she'd grown up thinking of her dad as being everything that was the opposite of her mom.

"Do you have any other stalls?" Tim asked as they walked out of the barn and over to the turnout paddocks.

"No," Amy replied. She looked at him in surprise. Something about his voice suggested that he had been hoping there would be more.

"I see," Tim said. He was quiet for a moment, fussing over Maddison and Sovereign, who had come up to the gate to check for treats. "What, er, what happened to Pegasus?" he asked.

Amy suddenly realized that her father didn't know that Pegasus had died. And one thing her mom had always told her was that her dad had been devoted to his great show-jumping partner. Her mom's voice came back to her now. "I think that was one of the things that hurt your father the most after the accident. He couldn't bear the thought that he had hurt Pegasus."

"Um —" She faltered, looking at Lou for support.

"He died in October," Lou said, coming over to join them. "We had to put him to sleep. He had cancer."

Amy looked at her father's stunned expression. For a long moment, he didn't speak.

"In October," he said at last. "So I'm four months too late to see my boy."

Amy knew how he felt. Pegasus had been a horse of a lifetime. Once you loved him, you loved him forever. She glanced around at Lou to see if she understood, too, but her sister's lips had tightened.

"Yes, I'm afraid you are," she said briefly.

Tim didn't seem to notice the coolness in Lou's voice. "I'd hoped —" his voice trailed off. For a moment he stared out across the fields, and then he gave a slight shake of his head and turned. "I have an idea," he said. "Why don't we all go out for a ride together? It will be just like old times."

Amy's eyes flew to her sister's face.

"I — I don't ride anymore," Lou said quickly.

Tim frowned. "What do you mean, you don't ride? Since when?"

Lou looked at the ground. "Since your accident."

"Since my accident?" Tim echoed. He stared at Lou. "Lou, is that really true?"

Lou nodded.

"But you were on a horse before you could walk!" Tim exclaimed. A frown deepened the lines in his face. "Are you scared because of what happened to me?"

"No!" Lou said looking up, her cheeks flaming.

"It was an accident, Lou," Tim said, his voice softening. "Nothing more. An accident that was my fault."

"I am not scared!" Lou exclaimed hotly.

Before Tim could say anything more, there was the sound of the phone ringing. "I'll get it," Lou said, sounding relieved.

"That's OK," Amy said. "Ben or Ty will get it."

But Lou was already hurrying toward the house.

"I think I've upset her," Tim said.

"She's just a bit weird about the riding thing," Amy said.

"Do you think she's scared?" Tim asked.

"I — I don't think so," Amy replied. "I mean, she's never said so."

Tim sighed. "I'd better go after her."

Amy followed him to the kitchen. Lou was just putting the phone down. "It was a prospective client," she said before Amy could ask. "Now," she said briskly, starting to clear away the coffee cups as if nothing had happened, "we should start thinking about what we want to eat. There's Grandpa's baked ham or a lasagne I cooked yesterday afternoon, which would —"

"Forget about lunch, Lou," Tim interrupted her. "Look, I'm sorry if I upset you just now. It was just such a shock. You used to love riding so much."

"That was then," Lou said briefly. She saw Tim about to open his mouth again. "Please," she said, holding up her hand. "I'd really rather not talk about it. Now," she said, pulling the fridge door open, "what can I get you for lunch?"

Chapter Seven

Ty and Ben joined them for lunch, which lightened the atmosphere considerably. As Tim chatted about horses, Amy felt herself starting to warm to him slightly. Maybe the day wasn't going to turn out quite as badly as she'd imagined.

However, when the last coffee cup had been drained and Ty and Ben went back outside, silence fell. Amy shifted in her chair, wishing she could leave the room.

"So," Tim said somewhat awkwardly, "here we are."

"Yes," Lou said with a pulled smile. "Here we are."

Amy started counting the knots in the wooden table-top.

"Daddy," Lou said suddenly. "Can I ask you something?"

"Sure, fire away," Tim replied, leaning back in his chair.

Picking up a petal that had fallen from one of the flowers, Lou passed it from hand to hand. "Why didn't you ever come and find me?" she asked at last. She looked up at him. "I mean, you knew where I was at school in England. Even if you didn't want to see Mom, why didn't you come and see me?"

Amy looked up, startled. She was surprised Lou would ask such a pointed question.

"You stayed at school in England?" Tim said, looking shocked.

"You didn't know?" Lou said slowly.

"No," Tim said. "I just assumed you'd moved to Virginia with your mom."

Lou shook her head. "I stayed at my boarding school. I was sure you'd come and find me. I wanted to stay there so you'd know where I was. So you'd know I was there for you."

"I didn't realize," Tim said, staring at her. "I wrote to your mom about a year after she moved here. I wanted to know how you all were. She wrote back and said everyone was fine, but she never told me that you were still in England."

"She didn't tell you?" Lou echoed, shock on her face. "But why?"

Tim shook his head. "I don't know. Maybe she was hesitant for us to spend time together when she was so far away. Your mother was always protective. She had her weaknesses just like everyone else."

Amy stared. "No, she didn't!" she exclaimed. "How could you say that? Mom knew how much you meant to Lou. She'd never hurt Lou just to get back at you!"

A look of bewilderment fell across Tim's face. "Amy, I didn't —" he said, reaching for her hand.

Amy jerked her hand away. "Don't you dare say anything against Mom!" she said, jumping angrily to her feet. "You were the one who left!"

"I know, I know," Tim said. "I was just trying to help Lou to understand. I didn't mean to upset you. I'm sorry."

Amy felt like picking up the nearby vase of flowers and throwing it at him. She felt like throwing everything in the room at him, but seeing Lou's shocked face, she fought the urge. She wouldn't ruin this day for Lou — she wouldn't. "Fine, it's fine," she said, having to force the words out through clenched teeth.

"Can I get anyone a drink?" Lou said in an obvious attempt to diffuse the situation.

"Thank you. Just a glass of water," Tim said.

"Amy?"

Amy shook her head. She might have managed to stop herself from losing her temper, but right now she couldn't stand to spend another minute in her father's company. "I'm going to go help Ty and Ben," she said, making for the door.

Feeling almost too angry to speak, Amy marched up the yard. She stopped by the tack room, but she knew she was in no state of mind to work a horse or even to groom one. Instead she went into the feed room and started to fill the hay nets, stuffing great handfuls of hay into them with enormous force. *I hate him, I hate him, I hate him,* she repeated over and over again in her head as she remembered his words.

"So what's up with you?" Amy turned and saw that Ty was watching her from the doorway.

"I don't want to talk about it," she said, almost spitting each word out.

"Is it your dad?" Ty said.

"What do you think?" Amy snapped.

Ty ignored her harsh words. "I thought you seemed to be getting along OK with him earlier," he said, coming over to her.

"Well, you're wrong!" Amy almost shouted. She saw Ty's shocked expression. "Look, I'm sorry," she said, raking her hands through her long hair. "I don't mean to take it out on you. It's just something he said. I think I need to be alone for a while." She managed a small smile. "Maybe I'll just beat up on this hay some more."

Ty nodded understandingly. "OK," he said, squeezing her arm. "But if you need to talk" — his green eyes searched hers — "you know I'm always here."

"I know," she said with a grateful smile.

Ty turned to go.

"Thanks, Ty," she called after him.

He threw a smile over his shoulder. "Any time."

After filling the hay nets, Amy set to work brushing the dried mud off the outdoor blankets. It was hard work, and she was soon red in the face and dripping with sweat, but by the time all the blankets had been cleaned up, she was feeling much better. It didn't matter what her dad said. He was only here for the weekend. She didn't have to see him again.

She was just hanging up the last blanket when she heard footsteps outside.

"Amy?" Lou called.

Amy went out. Lou and Tim were standing there.

"Dad's got to go in a few minutes," Lou said.

"But I'm going to come and visit again tomorrow," Tim said. "I'd love to see you ride then."

Amy nodded but didn't speak.

"I meant to ask you at lunchtime," Tim said. "Do you compete in any shows?"

"Yes," Amy replied briefly. "I could have gone to one tomorrow." She managed to stop herself from adding that it would have been a million times better than spending the day with him.

Tim smiled. "I'm impressed. I wouldn't have missed a competition for anyone when I was younger — not for anything."

Amy didn't reply. The silence grew.

"Well — I'd better go," Tim said at last.

"Come and see Daddy off, Amy." Lou gave Amy a pleading look, and Amy reluctantly joined her sister at their father's side.

"Is it OK if I come about ten again?" Tim asked as he opened the door of his rented car.

"Fine," Lou said.

For a moment it looked like Tim was going to step forward and hug her, but then he seemed to change his mind. "See you tomorrow," he said, and getting into the car, he shut the door and drove away.

"If I never see him again after this weekend, it will be too soon!" Amy exclaimed as his car disappeared out of sight. She turned to Lou. "Can't you go out for the day with him or something tomorrow? Or can't I go to the show? He doesn't need to see me again."

"Yes, he does," Lou said firmly. "You need to get to know each other."

"If he's going to say those sorts of things about Mom, then I don't think I want to," Amy muttered.

Lou sighed. "Amy, I know today might not have been quite as perfect as we'd been imagining."

"As you'd been imagining," Amy corrected her quickly. She frowned. "Anyway, why wasn't it perfect for you?"

Lou looked embarrassed. "I suppose it just didn't go exactly the way I thought it would. But anyway, that doesn't matter," she said, her voice suddenly brisk. "It'll get better. I know it will. We just need some time to get to know each other again." She looked beseechingly at Amy. "Please, Amy. We've got to keep trying."

Amy looked at her for a long moment and then gave in. "OK, OK," she said. "I'll see him tomorrow if it makes you happy."

❧

Amy was filling Jake's water bucket at the tap near the house when Tim arrived the next morning. The back door opened. "You're early," Lou said, coming out. "It's only nine-thirty."

Tim smiled. "Well, I didn't see the point of staying in my hotel when I could be here with you." He lifted a hand in Amy's direction. "Hey, Amy."

Amy felt like scowling, but knowing Lou was watching, she forced a smile onto her face. "Hi," she said coldly.

"Have you had breakfast? Can I get you anything to eat or drink?" Lou asked.

"No food," Tim said. "The hotel served an enormous breakfast. But maybe some coffee?"

"Sure," Lou said. "Come on in." She glanced across at Amy. "Are you coming, too?"

Amy shook her head. "I can't. There's still lots to do." She saw Lou's eyes start to narrow. "Ben's at the show. I can't make Ty do everything on his own," she said quickly, trying to ignore the guilty feeling that was sneaking up on her.

"If you're that busy, I can do without the coffee," Tim said suddenly. "Why don't I give you a hand?"

It wasn't what Amy had been intending at all. She started to shake her head. "It's OK, don't worry."

"It's not a problem," Tim interrupted, coming toward her. "Just tell me what to do." He smiled. "To tell you the truth, I'll enjoy it. I hate being away from my yard when I'm on business." He glanced back at Lou. "You'll come and help, too, won't you, Lou?"

Lou hesitated. "I guess so," she said at last.

"So what do you want me to do?" Tim asked Amy as Lou went inside to change.

Amy swallowed. She hadn't really been telling the truth when she'd said there was lots to do. Knowing that Ben would be away at the show, Ty had come to work early, and most of the basic chores, like mucking out and sweeping the yard, were just about done.

Tim misunderstood her silence. "I'm not proud. I don't mind mucking out or scrubbing buckets."

"Maybe you could groom a couple of horses for us," Amy faltered.

"Sure," he agreed easily. "Show me which ones."

Cringing inwardly, Amy led the way to the tack room. She had a feeling that her father knew enough about the running of a yard to have guessed that she had just been trying to use her supposed busyness as an excuse to get out of spending time with him. *Well, so what if he does know,* she thought, trying to ignore the guilt snaking through her brain. *It's not as if I care what he thinks.*

But it was nice of him to offer to help, a small voice said in her head.

Amy ignored it. "Here's a grooming kit," she said. "Could you groom Rosie and Jake for me? The Appaloosa filly and the Clydesdale," she explained.

Tim nodded. "Their halters?" he said.

"Hanging outside their stalls," Amy replied. She frowned. "Maybe I better put Rosie's on. She came here to be cured of being head shy, and although she's getting better, she's only used to being haltered by me or Ty at the moment."

"Well, if you think she's ready, I don't mind having a go," Tim offered, looking at Rosie. "She's going to have to get used to other people handling her as well. Why not let me have a try?"

Every fiber in Amy's being wanted to object. Heartland was hers and her mom's. She didn't want to let her father have anything to do with it. But how could she say that?

"I'm not going to get worried if she goes up in the air or anything," Tim said.

"OK," Amy reluctantly agreed, unable to think of an excuse.

They walked over to the stall. As usual, Rosie's head was lowered, her eyes half closed. "Is she OK?" Tim said.

"Yeah, she always stands like that," Amy said.

"She doesn't look right to me," Tim said.

"She's fine," Amy answered, her apprehension at her father handling Rosie making her curt.

Tim looked as if he was about to say something more, but then he seemed to change his mind. "Sorry," he said. "Of course you know your own horses best."

Amy nodded, but inside she felt a twinge of guilt. She couldn't deny that as much as she told herself that Rosie's quietness was just a personality trait, a feeling was still niggling her that something wasn't quite right with the filly.

Tim took the halter off the door and went into the stall. Rosie backed off as he entered. "Hi, there, girl,"

Tim said softly. "You're a beauty, aren't you?" He didn't approach the filly but waited until she came to him.

With a snort, Rosie bent her head and snuffled at his hands.

"Now let's see about this halter," Tim said. Murmuring to her in a soft voice, he drew the noseband of the halter slowly but confidently over the filly's chestnut muzzle and fastened the strap behind her ears.

Amy tensed, waiting for an explosion, but none came. Rosie flinched slightly but stood still. "There's a good girl," Tim praised. He turned to Amy. "And you say she used to be badly head shy?"

Amy nodded.

"Then you've done an amazing job," Tim said.

Amy felt a wave of pride, but she squashed it. *You don't care what he thinks,* she reminded herself firmly. "I better get going with the rest of the grooming," she said and hurried away.

❧

Amy groomed Sundance and then went to find Lou to see if she could give her a hand turning Blackjack and Crispin out. But Lou was nowhere to be found. Feeling puzzled, Amy asked Ty if he knew where she was.

"She said something about getting some work done in the office," Ty said.

Amy went to the house. Why would Lou be working

like being handled. As she backed away, Amy sent her out around the ring. Ten minutes later, the filly was standing, letting Amy stroke her scar.

It was only then that Amy took her concentration off Rosie to look across at her father to see if he understood. "See?"

Tim nodded. "Yeah, I do. I use the same principles when I'm training — reward the behavior you want, ignore the behavior you don't. I used them when I was show jumping, too."

He saw the surprised expression on Amy's face. "Why are you so shocked? Did you think I used to beat my horses over the fences?" As her face flushed guiltily, he shook his head. "Amy, you knew Pegasus. Can you imagine how far I'd have gotten if I'd tried to use force with him?" He shook his head. "That was one amazing horse. If you asked him to do something he'd try his heart out for you. If you tried to force him," he smiled a faint smile, "well, you'd more than likely end up on the ground."

"He was always like that," Amy said, feeling her eyes suddenly well up with tears, "right till the end."

Tim cleared his throat. "How did he die?" he asked. "I mean, I know you said it was cancer, but what happened?"

"It was after Mom's accident." Amy swallowed. "He — he was fine for a few months, and then it was like he realized she wasn't coming back. He stopped eating, and eventually he just got too weak and — and the tumor was so big," she took a deep breath, "we had to put him down." Blinking her tears back, she looked at her father. His face was full of emotion.

Tim rubbed a hand over his forehead. "You miss him a lot?"

Amy had to force the words past the lump in her throat. "More than I can say," she whispered painfully.

"Me, too," Tim said, his eyes meeting hers. "I've missed him for twelve years."

Amy stared at him as the truth suddenly hit her. He was the one person in the world who could understand how she felt. He'd loved the great gray horse as much as she had. "I — I could show you where he's buried if you like," she whispered.

As soon as the words were out of her mouth she began to regret them. Pegasus's burial spot was a very special place to her. But it was too late. The offer had been made.

"Yes, I'd like that," Tim said quietly. "Thank you."

"I'll just put Rosie back first," Amy said.

As she led the filly to one of the turnout paddocks, her mind raced. She was about to show Pegasus's grave to her father. She reached deep inside herself and tried to dredge up the anger she usually felt toward him, but it had gone.

So how did she feel about him then?

I don't know, she thought in confusion.

Reaching the paddock gate, she unclipped Rosie's lead rope. The filly trotted over to the stream that ran through the field and began to graze under one of the willow trees.

"She always grazes in that spot," Amy told Tim.

He smiled. "It's amazing how horses have their favorite places to eat. Maybe she thinks the grass tastes better there."

Amy half wished that they could stay there talking about Rosie, but she could sense her father's restlessness. She swallowed. There was no going back now. "Pegasus's field is over there," she said.

Chapter Eight

Tim followed her down the drive to the empty paddock. The winter's rain and lack of grazing had left the grass green. In the middle of the paddock stood a single young oak tree. It was silhouetted against the sky, fresh leaf buds bursting out on its slender branches.

Opening the gate, Amy walked over to it. At the foot of the tree was a mound of earth. Once bare soil, it now had a thin coat of grass seedlings.

Amy didn't need to say a word. Tim knelt beside the mound and touched it. For a moment, he didn't speak.

"I remember when you were tiny," he said at last to Amy. "You refused to be left behind when your mom, Lou, and I went for rides, so I'd sit you in front of me on Pegasus. I swear he was a different horse when he knew you were on his back. Not once did he buck or carry on like he used to when I was riding on my own."

Amy nodded. "I remember that he used to let me play around his feet when Mom was grooming him or working in his stall. Once I braided his tail with lots of different-colored ribbons. I couldn't wait to be big enough to groom him myself."

Tim smiled at her. "He was a horse in a million."

"The best," Amy agreed.

"So brave," Tim said. His eyes clouded with memories. "Any other horse would have refused to jump off such a tight angle, but he didn't. He trusted me, and he tried to do it —" He broke off, pinching the bridge of his nose.

Amy knew he'd been talking about the night of his accident — that night at the World Championships when he had turned Pegasus too sharply into a fence and Pegasus had caught the top pole between his legs and come crashing down.

Tim took a deep breath. "It doesn't matter how many years pass, it doesn't get any easier." He looked at her. "But he was a lucky horse to have you and your mom to look after him."

Amy didn't know what to say. Part of her wanted to shout out that he had no right to say such a thing, that he should have never left if he felt that way about Pegasus —

about them. But at the same time there was no denying
the love and loss in her father's eyes. He saved her the
need to speak by quickly squeezing her shoulder.

"I'm glad you loved him, too, Amy," he said.

And in that moment Amy gave up her will to fight
him. Her father had loved Pegasus as much as she had,
and for now that was enough. Her eyes met his. "I did,"
she whispered. "I still do."

They stood side by side, each looking at the grave,
their love for Pegasus wrapping around them, drawing
them together.

Tim crouched down. "Sleep well, old friend," he whispered, touching the grassy mound. "Sleep well."

After a long moment, he stood up. "Well," he said, his
tone lightening, "I guess I shouldn't hold you up any
longer. Not when there's still so much to do."

Amy glanced at him. The hint of a smile was flickering
at the corners of her father's mouth. Almost before she
realized what she was doing, she had smiled back. "I
think we'll manage," she admitted rather sheepishly.

"You know, I meant what I said yesterday," Tim said
as they walked back across the paddock together. "I
would love to go out for a ride."

"Well, we can," Amy said, shutting the gate behind
them. "We could go after lunch."

"Do you think there's any point in trying to persuade
Lou to come with us?" Tim said.

Amy shook her head.

Tim sighed. "She used to love horses — and riding — so much."

"Not anymore," Amy said.

Her father seemed to catch the slight note of wistfulness in her voice. "And that causes a problem between you?"

Amy hesitated. Although she felt a whole lot closer to her father than she had at the start of the day, she didn't want to discuss Lou and her attitude toward horses with him. Amy sensed that whatever she said would feel like a betrayal of her sister. "Not really," she lied. She quickly moved the conversation in a different direction. "So, um, what did you think of Rosie?" she asked as they approached the paddock where the Appaloosa filly was turned out. She was still in the same place by the stream, but now instead of grazing she was nibbling the bare arching branches of the willow tree.

She felt her father look at her for a moment, but then he went along with the change of subject. "You've done a wonderful job on her," he said, studying the filly. "To go from not wanting to be haltered to behaving as well as she did today — and in just a week — well, that's a fantastic achievement." As he spoke, Rosie lifted her head and circled it in the air. Tim frowned. "I don't like that head shaking, though. You're going to have to work on that. And there's something else. I can't put my finger on it — maybe it's her quietness — but something doesn't seem quite right with her."

Though Amy felt slightly put out at the less than complete praise, deep down she was glad her father was being honest about what he thought. She knew that she would never lie about her observations of a horse just to make someone feel better, and it made her respect her father more to realize that he wouldn't, either. "I know," she admitted. "I guess I've sort of been feeling the same myself."

"Have you had her checked by a vet?" Tim asked, stopping at the fence and looking at the filly.

"Yes, she was examined by a vet before she came here," Amy replied. "He gave her the all clear, but the next day when her owner tried to put the halter on, Rosie was so agitated she reared up in the stable and hit her head on the wooden partition. After that, she became totally impossible to halter, and that's when the owner called us."

Tim frowned. "Maybe she did herself some damage when she reared. That was after the vet's visit, right?" Amy nodded. "If her behavior got worse after that, maybe she injured herself then."

Of course! Amy stared at him. Why hadn't she thought of that? "That could explain why she's been shaking her head!" she exclaimed. "And why she's been so quiet."

"She could have a small fracture," Tim said. He

frowned suddenly. "You know what, I bet that's a basket willow she's chewing." He started to climb the fence.

"Basket willow?" Amy echoed, climbing after him.

Tim strode across the field, only slowing down as he reached the filly. "I knew it!" he said, examining the tree. "Basket willow," he said, turning to Amy. "It's a natural painkiller. Horses often graze on it when they're in pain." He saw her surprised expression. "Don't tell me your mom didn't teach you that?"

"No, she didn't," Amy replied. "How do you know about it?"

"An old horseman told me about it," Tim replied. He patted Rosie, who was snuffling hopefully at his pockets. "Poor girl, I reckon you've got a headache." His fingers stroked gently up her face, examining the bones on either side. When he reached a spot just above her left eye, Rosie tossed her head. Tim tried again, but every time his fingers reached the same spot, Rosie threw her head in the air. "Yeah, there's definitely something bothering her," Tim said. "If I were you, I'd get her checked over again."

Amy nodded. "I'll call Scott." She stroked the Appaloosa's nose. "We'll find out what's wrong with you, girl. I promise."

❦

When Amy telephoned Scott, he agreed to come over the next morning. "My dad thinks Rosie might have a small fracture," Amy said. My dad. Suddenly, she realized that it was the first time in his visit that she had said those two words aloud. It felt strange to say them — strange but good, she decided. She caught Tim's eye and realized that the words hadn't escaped him, either. He was smiling at her.

"I wish you were staying longer," she said impulsively as she replaced the receiver.

"Well, I'm here for a week," Tim said. "I've got business to attend to, and then I fly home on Saturday night. I could come and visit some more. I'd have suggested it from the start, but I thought it might be best to see how the weekend went first. But if you'd like me to visit in the afternoons when I've finished with work, then I'd love to."

Lou came into the kitchen.

"Lou," Amy said quickly, "Daddy's going to come and visit every day this week."

"That's nice," Lou said with a smile, but there was a strangely flat note in her voice.

"Amy's just been showing me Pegasus's field," Tim said.

Lou stared at Amy. Amy understood her astonishment. Lou knew how special Pegasus's grave was to her. Amy wished she could explain how Tim understood and shared her love for Pegasus, shared it in a way that no one else could. But with him standing there, she couldn't put those thoughts into words.

"And I watched a join up," Tim went on. "It was fantastic." He looked proudly at Amy. "Amy's got a real gift with horses."

Happiness flooded through Amy. "I'm not the only one." She turned to Lou. "Daddy's helped me figure out what's causing Rosie to shake her head. We think she's injured her head."

"Well, I'm glad that you think you've got the problem solved," Lou said abruptly.

The tension in Lou's voice was obvious. Amy frowned. What was the matter with her? Wondering if Lou was feeling a little left out, she turned to Tim. "Lou noticed the head shaking before any of us," she said, wanting to include Lou. "The first day I worked Rosie, she saw it. And she noticed that Rosie seemed quiet."

"Well, it looks like your instincts were probably right, Lou." Tim smiled at her. "Now, Amy and I have decided to go out riding this afternoon," he went on. "Why don't you join us?"

But Lou shook her head. "I'm busy. I want to get this business plan finished so that Grandpa and Amy can see it tonight. In fact," she cleared her throat, "I'm afraid I should get back to it now. I've got a lot to do."

And looking at the floor, she hurried out of the room.

❦

Amy and Tim took Moochie and Sundance out along one of the trails in the woods behind Heartland that afternoon. As they rode up the mountain, Tim talked about his business, importing and exporting young sports horses to and from Australia.

"I love it," he told her, his eyes gleaming. "You take a shaggy-coated, unbacked three-year-old that a buyer wouldn't look twice at, and twelve months down the line, you've got a healthy, well-mannered young horse."

"Do you back them yourself?" Amy asked.

"No, the old injury to my neck won't stand too much falling off," Tim said. "But I supervise. I've got a staff of ten." He smiled. "You'll have to come visit."

"I'd like to," Amy said, smiling at him. She saw a fallen tree trunk on the track ahead and shortened her reins. "Watch Sundance jump this!"

Sundance flew over the log.

"What do you think?" Amy said, cantering up to Moochie.

Tim was shaking his head. "You're so like your mom," he said. "Watching you ride is like seeing her all over again."

Amy reined Sundance in. *Like Mom. He thinks I'm like Mom,* she thought. No compliment could have been better.

She glanced across at him. His eyes were warm, and suddenly a question burst from her. "Why did you leave us?"

As soon as the words left her lips, she felt the blood rush to her cheeks. She looked down at Sundance's mane, feeling very embarrassed.

For a moment there was silence, and then she heard Tim sigh. "Cowardice, weakness," he said quietly. "I just couldn't cope. You have to remember that at the time no one was sure if I would ever walk again, and my career as a show jumper was over. I'd always been so strong, so fit. I felt like everything I knew, everything I was, fell away from me when I took that fall. I felt that your mom would be better off without me — that if she stayed with me, it would be out of pity. That was something I couldn't handle. That's why I left."

"You disappeared," Amy said, trying to keep the accusatory tone out of her voice.

Tim's eyes met hers. "Do you think I could have gone if I'd stayed to say good-bye? Amy — you, your mom, Lou, you were the three most precious things in the world to me. There's no way that I could have looked at your faces and then turned and walked away."

"If that's true, then you shouldn't have gone!" Amy cried. "We were a family. Mom would have stayed with you. Not out of pity, out of love."

"I realized that after a while — that's when I got back

in touch with your mom. I begged her to reconcile," Tim said. "But by then it was too late. Her pain was too deep." He shook his head, his face showing regret. "I'd always prided myself on being brave. But the moment I needed courage, it failed me. I can't believe I left you. It's a decision that will haunt me for the rest of my life."

Amy felt the anger leave her. He was sincere; she could hear it in his voice and see it in his face. "You've got Helena now," she said. "And Lily."

"Yes," Tim said, his eyes growing warm. "That's true."

Amy swallowed, wondering suddenly about the woman who had taken her mom's place. "What's Helena like?" she asked, trying to keep her voice casual.

If she was hoping for her dad to say that no one could compare to her mom, she was disappointed. "Wonderful," Tim said. "It was Helena who made me realize that I couldn't let the mistakes I'd made in the past determine the rest of my life. She helped me accept what had happened and move on. That's what your mom had done." He smiled. "I knew your mom would understand. When we were together she always used to say it was a waste of time to linger in the past — you should learn, move on, and —"

"Look to the good times ahead," Amy finished quietly. It was a saying that she knew well.

"That's right. Well, it's what I've tried to do. And" — Tim's eyes met hers — "what I'm going to try to do from now on."

❧

"You look like you had a good time," Ty commented as Amy came back into the stable after saying good-bye to her father.

"It was really great!" Amy said genuinely.

"So maybe your dad isn't so bad after all?" Ty said, coming into the stall.

"I think that's a fair statement," Amy said. She put an arm over Sundance's back and smiled radiantly. "It's like all these questions in my mind have finally been answered. I understand at last. And what I don't understand, I'm willing to let go. But the best part is that he understands me. I feel like" — she looked at Ty to see if he knew what she was getting at — "well, like I belong. "

"That's wonderful, Amy. I'm happy for you," Ty said, and he leaned forward and gently kissed her on the forehead.

Amy smiled at him and sighed happily. It had been such an unexpectedly good day.

❧

At six-thirty, Jack's car drew up in front of the house. Amy and Lou both went to meet him.

"How was your weekend, Grandpa?" Lou asked.

"Great," Jack said. "But more important" — his eyes searched their faces — "how was yours?"

"Fine," Lou said. "It was fine." There was a slight hesitation in her voice.

Jack frowned. "But not like you'd hoped?"

"It was just fine," Lou said quickly. "Wasn't it, Amy?"

"Yeah," Amy said. "It was — " she was about to say "fabulous" but stopped herself. She didn't want to hurt Grandpa's feelings by going on about how great it had been to see Daddy. "It was OK," she said. "And, well," she looked nervously at Grandpa, wondering how he'd react to what she was about to tell him, "Daddy's going to come and visit this week after he's finished work in the afternoons."

Grandpa's mouth tightened, and for a moment he became very quiet. "Well, if it makes you both happy, I'm glad," he said at last.

Amy knew how hard it must have been for him to say those words. "It does," she said gratefully. "Doesn't it, Lou?"

"Of course," Lou said lightly. "Now, Grandpa," she said, changing the subject, "you should come inside. I've finished the business plan, and when you've had a chance to relax I'd really like to go through it with you and Amy. Then I can take it into the bank tomorrow — if you both agree to it, of course," she added quickly. "We need to get the bid in as quickly as possible — before the Grants submit theirs."

They went into the house. Grandpa changed and then

came down to the kitchen, where Amy was helping Lou prepare pasta for supper.

"OK, let's have a look at this plan," he said, sitting down at the table.

Amy added the remaining ingredients to the bolognese sauce, leaving it to simmer on the stove, and sat down beside him.

Lou handed each of them a copy of the business plan. "After you've looked through it, we can discuss it," she said.

Amy ran her eyes over the paper. There were lots of figures. Initial outlay, overheads, net profit. The words spun through her brain.

"You can see it's going to be profitable," Lou said after a few minutes. "And it could bring in a regular income, which is exactly what we need to support Amy's rehabilitation work." Her eyes shone. "If it turns out to be a success it could fund extensions to Heartland. We might be able to add another barn, another training ring. We could do so much more to help."

Amy bit her lip. Lou had listened to Amy's concerns about how many hours the horses could work. On paper she could see that there were no arguments. It did sound like a good idea.

"It's a big risk, Lou," Jack said, looking at the amount of money they would have to borrow.

"Yes, but risks are all part of a good business plan,"

Lou said. She looked at him. "It will work, Grandpa," she said. "It really will."

"All right," Jack said slowly. "If Amy agrees, then you can submit the plan."

Both he and Lou looked at Amy.

"Well?" Lou asked her hopefully.

Amy took a deep breath. She didn't want to upset Lou at this point in time. "OK," she said extremely reluctantly. "I agree."

The look that crossed Lou's face almost made the sacrifice worth it.

"It's the right decision, Amy," Lou said, in delight. "You just wait and see!"

Chapter Nine

"So how did Ben do at the show?" Soraya said to Amy on the bus the next morning on the way to school.

"He won his class," Amy told her. "He was thrilled."

"Cool!" Soraya said. She grinned. "Maybe I'll have to come over to congratulate him."

Amy grinned back. "And suggest that he take you out for a victory dinner?"

"Of course," Soraya said, arching her eyebrows. "I mean, it's the perfect excuse." She smiled. "Well, apart from the riding school plan, it sounds like you had a pretty cool weekend."

"I did," Amy said, her eyes glowing with the memory. "It ended up being really good seeing my dad and talking to him at last."

"And he's coming to visit all week?" Soraya said.

"Every day," Amy replied.

"What did your grandpa say when he found out?" Soraya asked. "I bet he wasn't exactly delighted."

"Well," Amy admitted, "I think he wishes Daddy had just stayed away."

"It must be really hard for him," Soraya said. "What about Lou? She must be pleased."

"If she is, she's got a funny way of showing it," Amy said. She saw Soraya's intrigued expression and shook her head. "She was in a totally odd mood yesterday. It was almost like she was avoiding Daddy. When he was helping in the yard she went and worked inside. I thought she'd be pleased that I was getting along so well with him, but she seemed almost angry."

"Maybe she was feeling left out," Soraya suggested. "I mean, if you and your dad were talking horses — well, that's not really Lou's thing, is it?"

Amy frowned. "I kind of wondered that, too." She thought about the weekend. "I guess we did talk about horsey things a lot." Suddenly, she remembered the argument between Lou and Tim on Saturday. "Dad's got this theory that Lou won't ride because she's scared."

"Do you think he's right?" Soraya asked.

"Well, Lou says she isn't scared, and she certainly doesn't act scared around the horses, but it is odd that she won't ride." Amy's eyes widened. "Maybe that's why she's avoiding Daddy — she *is* scared, and she's afraid he'll make her admit it."

Soraya grinned. "Careful, Amy. You're in danger of becoming a human psychologist as well as a horse one."

"But I could be right," Amy said.

Just then Matt got on the bus, and Amy dropped the subject. Since Matt had started going out with Ashley, she had felt weird talking about personal stuff when he was around.

"How was your weekend?" Soraya asked him as he sat down.

"Not that great," Matt replied. He sighed. "I broke up with Ashley."

Amy and Soraya both stared at him. "You dumped Ashley?" Amy exclaimed. That was a first in their high school's history. Ashley Grant usually did the dumping.

"Yeah," Matt said glumly. "She kept trying to run my life. It was like I didn't have a life outside of dating her."

"Wow!" Amy said, impressed. "I bet that caught her off guard."

"She did seem to take it kind of hard," Matt said quietly.

"And how are you about it?" Soraya asked him, her brown eyes concerned.

"I'm fine," Matt muttered.

"You are better off without her," Amy said. *"Ow!"* she

exclaimed as Soraya elbowed her sharply. She glared at her friend, but Soraya was looking at Matt's face.

"You really liked her, didn't you, Matt?" Soraya said softly.

"Yeah, I guess I did," Matt admitted, and for the first time Amy took in the sadness in his eyes. He sighed. "I know you two don't get along with her, but she's not as bad as she seems — really she's not. When you get her on her own, she's really sweet — vulnerable even. She hasn't had it easy, you know. Her mom had her riding in shows every weekend from the time she was five."

"My heart bleeds for her," Amy said sarcastically. "Come on. I helped my mom with the horses when I could barely walk!"

"Don't be so harsh, Amy. Your mom never treated you like a marionette," Matt said, and Amy immediately felt bad. "Ashley's always had to look good, win ribbons, get her photo in the papers," Matt went on. "That's what her mom and dad have always expected, and so that's what she does."

Amy didn't say anything. OK, maybe Ashley hadn't had it totally easy, but she still had major attitude. However, she could see that Matt was upset, and so she didn't say anything else about Ashley. She squeezed his arm. "You did the right thing," she said comfortingly. "You shouldn't let her boss you around."

"I know." Matt said. He shook his head. "I just wish I didn't feel so bad."

♊

When Amy got back to Heartland that afternoon, Tim had already arrived. He was helping Ty groom Jake. "Hey, there!" he called as she walked up the drive.

That's my dad, Amy thought, looking at him, his jeans dusty, a grooming brush in his hand. It was weird seeing him doing stuff at Heartland, but a good sort of weird.

"Hi," she said, going over. "You're here early."

"I finished work sooner than I expected," Tim said, "so I came over to see if I could lend a hand."

"We've been busy," Ty said. "Scott x-rayed Rosie after lunch."

"Did he find anything?" Amy asked quickly.

"Yeah, a hairline fracture just above one eye," Ty replied. "It'll heal on its own, but until it does he's given us some painkillers for her. I suggested that we feed her comfrey to speed the healing, and he agreed. We should also massage around the area with lavender oil to help relax her and ease her headache, but we need to be careful to avoid the exact spot."

"Have you told Sheri?" Amy asked.

"Yeah, she was really pleased that we'd figured out what the problem was. Scott said that the fracture should heal fairly quickly so she should be able to start working Rosie in about a month," Ty said.

"Great." Amy said, feeling relieved. Rosie still had to get better, but at least they knew what the problem was now. "Where are Lou and Grandpa?"

"Jack's out," Tim replied. "Lou's inside working."

"OK," Amy said. "I'll go get changed."

She walked toward the house, wondering whether her suspicions and her dad's were true. Was Lou avoiding their father because she was scared of riding?

She found her sister sitting at the kitchen table with the account books and her laptop open in front of her.

"What are you doing in here?" Amy asked.

"What does it look like?" Lou said shortly. "I'm working."

"But I thought you'd finished the business plan," Amy said. "Didn't you say you were going to drop it off at the bank this morning?"

"Yes, and I did," Lou said. "But I've been so busy with the business plan that I've gotten really behind with the accounts." She ran a hand through her hair. "And I'm not going to catch up if you stand here chatting with me."

"Sorry for breathing," Amy muttered, heading for her room. But just before she reached the door, she stopped. She had to say something. "Lou, I don't get it," she said. "I thought you'd be pleased that Daddy was here. I thought you'd want to spend as much time with him as possible."

"I do," Lou said, but Amy had noticed the moment's hesitation before she spoke. "But there's still work to do." Lou bent her head over her laptop. "I'll see Daddy when I'm done."

Amy spoke impulsively. "Is it because you're —" She broke off, suddenly remembering how touchy Lou had been when Tim had asked her whether she was scared. She and Lou had been getting along well. Did she really want to start an argument with her now?

"Because I'm what?" Lou said, looking up with a frown.

Amy hesitated for a moment and then shook her head. "It doesn't matter," she said, deciding against pursuing her question. She headed for the stairs. "I'm going to get changed."

As Amy pulled on her old jeans she remembered that she wanted to call Mrs. Newhart to ask if Jo could ride Feather. She went to the office and picked up the phone. Her mouth felt dry. She wasn't looking forward to the conversation, but Ty was right, they needed to find out how Feather would behave with Jo.

Donna Newhart answered.

Amy quickly explained why she was calling. "He's

been really good since he got here," she said. "He hasn't done a thing wrong. I'm as sure as I can be that he's safe."

There was silence from Mrs. Newhart's end of the phone.

"Mrs. Newhart?" Amy said at last.

"OK," Mrs. Newhart agreed reluctantly. "If you think he's safe, then Jo-Ann can ride him." A note of pleading entered her voice. "But, please — don't let anything happen to her."

❧

Half an hour later, Jo came walking up the drive. "I can't believe Mom said I can actually ride Feather again!" she exclaimed, dumping her bike and racing over to where Amy was grooming Rosie. "Can I go and tack him up right now?"

"OK," Amy said, with a smile.

Within ten minutes, Jo had her helmet on and was riding Feather around the ring.

"He looks fine," Tim said to Amy as they watched together from the gate.

"I know," Amy said, looking at the pretty Arabian pony. "He's been like this ever since he got here. He hasn't acted up at all."

"Perhaps something just spooked him that day you saw him," Tim suggested.

Amy thought back and frowned. "He didn't look as if

there was anything he was afraid of," she said, remembering how Feather had slowed down and tried to pull to the gate before he had finally reared.

"Well, he looks great now," Tim commented as Jo moved Feather into a smooth trot.

"Yeah," Amy said. She knew she'd have felt better if it had been something that she'd done that had brought about his improvement. OK, they'd used T-touch on him and massaged him with violet leaf oil, but that was all. She looked at the gray pony as he trotted around the ring. *He is better, I'm certain he is,* she told herself, wishing she could shake off the slight doubt that lingered in her mind.

❧

The next morning Matt wasn't on the bus on the way to school. However, as Amy and Soraya made their way to their first class, he came jogging up behind them. "Hi, guys!" he said. "Scott gave me a ride."

Compared to the day before, he sounded really cheerful. Amy glanced at him, surprised. "You look happy."

Matt grinned. "Ashley called me last night. She said she's totally sorry for the way she treated me and that she'd like to give our relationship another try."

Amy and Soraya stared at him. "You didn't say yes, did you?" Amy said.

"Of course I did," Matt said. "It's going to be fine," he

said quickly, seeing their faces. "Ashley promised she won't be such a nag anymore."

Amy saw a faint blush creeping up his neck. "And what else did she say?"

Matt shrugged but was unable to keep the pleased grin off his face. "Oh, just some other stuff." He looked at them pleadingly. "Come on, you guys, be happy for me."

Soraya sighed. "OK, I guess we'll try."

As Amy was walking home from the bus stop, Lou's car came along the road. She stopped and opened the door. "Jump in," she said. "I'll give you a ride."

Amy tossed her backpack in and climbed in after it.

"So how's your day been?" Lou asked as they set off up the drive.

"OK, apart from the fact that Matt's dating Ashley again," Amy replied. "I don't know what he sees in her." She shook her head, not wanting to think about it. "Have you heard from the bank yet?"

"No," Lou replied. "But we shouldn't have to wait too long, although we're still in competition with Green Briar to get the land."

She parked the car, and they went into the kitchen together.

Grandpa was speaking on the phone. "OK," he was

saying. "I'll tell them." His voice was tense, and when he put the phone down without saying good-bye, Amy frowned.

"Who was that?" she asked.

Jack's face looked strained. "Your father," he said. "He can't make it here tonight. He has to see some clients."

"Oh," Amy said, feeling disappointed. Without saying another word, Jack strode out of the room. Amy sighed. "I wish Grandpa could get along with Daddy." Jack hadn't gone out the day before when Tim had been visiting, but he had stayed in the house and avoided any contact with his former son-in-law.

"I think that might be too much to ask," Lou said. "It's putting a real strain on him, having Daddy here all week."

There was a strange note in Lou's voice. Amy frowned. It almost sounded as if Lou was accusing her of not considering Grandpa's feelings. "You were the one who invited Daddy here in the first place, Lou!" she protested.

"I know," Lou said defensively. "I'm just saying that it's tough on Grandpa." She pushed her fingers through her hair. "You know, maybe we shouldn't have asked Daddy to come and visit us every day."

Amy was astonished. Was this Lou speaking? The Lou who had refused to rest until she got in contact with their father again? "I don't get you, Lou," she said. "You were the one who was desperate to see Daddy again, but now that he's here, you don't seem very happy."

"Of course I'm happy," Lou said quickly, heading for the stairs.

"No, you're not!" Amy said, in exasperation. "Lou — what's wrong?"

For a moment, she thought her sister was just going to ignore her, but then Lou stopped.

"I don't know," she said, in a voice so quiet that Amy could hardly hear her. Her shoulders sagged as she turned back. "It's just" — she seemed to be struggling to find the right words — "just that Daddy's visit isn't turning out like I imagined. We don't seem to have anything to say to each other anymore."

"You just need to get to know him again," Amy said. "Spend time with him."

"How can I when —" Lou broke off. "It doesn't matter," she said quickly. "Forget it."

"Lou," Amy began, stepping toward her in concern.

Lou shook her head and backed off. "I'm going to my room," she said, and with that she hurried up the stairs.

Amy stood there for a long moment and then slowly went upstairs herself. Grandpa's bedroom door was shut, and so was Lou's.

Amy sank down on her bed and buried her face in her hands. *I just want everyone to get along,* she thought in frustration. She sighed. *Yeah, like that was really going to happen.*

⋔

The atmosphere didn't improve. Lou seemed to grow more distant from their father with every day that passed, and Grandpa continued to avoid him. The only good thing, as far as Amy was concerned, was that Feather continued to behave, and on Friday she decided that she would invite Mrs. Newhart to come watch Jo riding him that weekend.

"At least if she sees him behaving it might make her feel happier about Jo riding him," Amy said to Tim as they rode Solo and Sundance back from the trails that afternoon.

As they dismounted, Lou's Honda came up the drive. She jumped out. Her eyes were shining, and her face was split by a huge grin. "We got the approval from the bank!" she cried, waving an envelope excitedly. "They've agreed to lend us the money!"

"Oh." Amy could see from Lou's sudden frown that this wasn't the reaction her sister had been wanting. "That's great, Lou." She made herself smile. "Really great," she added, trying to sound as if she meant it.

"Well done, Lou," Tim said. "I know you've put a lot of work into that plan."

"As soon as Grandpa signs the agreement, I can put in

an offer on the land," Lou said. "This will mean we'll have a regular income. We won't just be scraping by anymore. We'll be able to plan for the future. It will be wonderful for Heartland."

"I really hope so," Tim said.

The smile left Lou's face. "You — you don't think it is?"

"Well, as I've said, I don't think that you should rush into it," Tim said cautiously. "After all, it could really change things around here."

Amy saw a look of hurt flash through Lou's eyes. "Yes — for the better!"

"Lou," Tim began placatingly, "I'm just saying it's a big move. I know you've worked out the business side thoroughly. But have you really thought through what it will mean for Heartland?"

"Of course I have!" Lou snapped. "And I know it's a good idea!"

Just then, Grandpa came out of the house. It was clear that he had heard the raised voices. "What's going on?" he asked, taking in the scene.

Lou didn't answer. She marched past him, but not before Amy had caught the glint of tears in her eyes.

From the look that Grandpa shot Tim, it was obvious that he had seen them, too. "I don't know what you said to her," he said, advancing angrily on the younger man, "but I'm not going to stand by and see you upset my granddaughter." He glared at him icily. "I think you should leave now."

"No!" Amy protested, grabbing her father's arm. "Don't go."

"I think it might be for the best, Amy," Tim said quietly. "I don't want to cause problems for anyone. I'll call you."

"Grandpa!" Amy said, turning to him beseechingly. "Daddy didn't mean to upset Lou. All he said was that she should think carefully before making a decision that would change things around here. Lou just overreacted. It wasn't Daddy's fault!"

She saw the anger slowly fade from Grandpa's eyes. "I see," he said. He paused. "Very well, then, Tim, if you were just trying to help Lou consider the outcome of her riding school plan, then I" — he took a deep breath — "I apologize for overreacting myself. I guess I'm a little on edge at the moment."

Tim shook his head. "There's no need to apologize, Jack. I know you just want to protect Lou and Amy, and believe me, I'm grateful for that. It's just that I've had experience with riding schools, and I know how difficult it can be to make them profitable." He rubbed his temples. "Still, I understand it's not my place to give advice. I should have kept my reservations to myself."

The tension left Grandpa's shoulders. "No," he said.

"This riding school is a big decision. You were right to say what you thought. It's best to be honest."

"I know," Tim replied. "That's exactly how I feel — I want to rebuild my relationship with my daughters with honesty and trust. And" — his gaze met Grandpa's — "it would really mean a lot to me to know that I had your support, Jack."

Amy looked at Grandpa. He hesitated for a moment, but then he nodded. "You do."

"Thank you," Tim said quietly. "I appreciate that."

Amy felt a wave of relief. Although Grandpa wasn't offering her dad friendship, maybe the first step toward an understanding had been made.

"And now I think I've got some more apologizing to do," Tim said, looking toward the house.

Chapter Ten

Lou was in the kitchen, setting the table. Amy watched her as each plate hit the tabletop with a bang.

"Lou, I'm sorry," Tim said, going over to her. "I should have realized how much this riding school idea means to you, and I should have been more supportive. I just wanted you to think things over from every angle, and not just rush into making an offer."

"I have thought things over," Lou said through gritted teeth.

"Well, that's good," Tim shook his head. "Come on, Lou," he said gently. "Please, let's not argue. I've only got one more day left."

Lou walked across the room and hesitated for a moment. She walked over to the window and stood looking out for a couple of moments. Amy and Tim waited quietly for her to say something. Lou sighed and turned around. "OK, you're right," she said. "I'm sorry for storming off like that. It's just I'm sure that having a riding school will be a good move for Heartland."

"I understand that now," Tim said. For a moment, Amy thought he was going to put his arm around Lou, but then something seemed to stop him. "So — when will you put the offer in?" he asked.

"I'll call the Youngs now," Lou said. She glanced at Jack, who was standing by the door. "That is OK, isn't it Grandpa?"

Grandpa nodded, and he, Amy, and Tim sat down while Lou went to the office to phone. Amy chewed a jagged nail on her little finger. She couldn't believe that the whole riding school thing was actually going to happen. Heartland was going to change so much.

At last Lou came back into the room.

"Well, what did they say?" Amy demanded, seeing that her sister's face looked concerned.

"They've already had an offer," Lou said.

"It's Green Briar, I know it is!" Amy burst out.

"The Youngs wouldn't say who it was from," Lou said, "but I'm sure you're right. I upped our offer, so now we've just got to wait and see. We can't afford to go any higher."

"When will we know?" Jack asked.

"Within the next twenty-four hours," Lou said.

A̶lthough the next day was officially Ty's day off, he turned up in the morning as usual to help feed the horses and muck out the stalls. He could only stay for a few hours, though, because he had promised to do the grocery shopping for his mom.

Tim came over to say good-bye. "It was really good to meet you, Ty," he said warmly. "I appreciate you sharing your knowledge with me this week."

"Same here," Ty said with a smile. "I won't forget about basket willow." He glanced at Amy. "Call me tonight?"

She nodded. Although he didn't say it out loud, she knew he meant that he wanted her to call after her father had gone to let him know how she was dealing with everything. "I will."

Ty got into his truck, and Amy and her father watched him drive away.

"Nice guy," Tim said, shooting a sideways look at her.

Amy smiled. "Yes," she agreed. "He is."

"So, what's there to do?" Tim asked as they turned to walk back up the yard.

Amy began to list the jobs. "Finish the stalls, tidy the muck heap, sweep the yard, the barn, the feed room."

Tim smiled. "I get the picture. Fetch me a broom."

At eleven o'clock, Mrs. Newhart arrived. "Jo, your mom's here!" Amy called down the barn aisle to where Jo, who had been there a couple of hours, was grooming Feather.

"Oh, no," Jo groaned.

"There's nothing to worry about," Amy said briskly. "Get Feather tacked up and take him to the ring, but don't get on him until I'm there." She hoped that having something concrete to do would calm Jo's nerves.

Stowing her broom in the rack, Amy headed down the yard. Lou had come out of the kitchen and was talking to Jo's mother. As Amy approached them she saw that Mrs. Newhart's face was tense. "I wish I knew what to do," Amy heard her saying to Lou. "If anything were to happen to Jo-Ann, I'd never forgive myself." She shook her head. "I wish she wouldn't ride, but how can I stop her? She loves horses so much."

"It's really difficult." Amy heard a note of real sympathy in her sister's voice. "It must be awful for you."

"It is." Mrs. Newhart smiled gratefully at her. "You know, at all the other barns where Jo's ever ridden, they've just dismissed me as a crazy, neurotic mom, but I can't help it. After everything that's happened . . ." Her voice trailed off, and for a moment she looked almost embarrassed.

"It's OK," Lou said gently. "I understand." She looked

up and saw Amy standing there. "Is Feather ready?" she said, her voice regaining its usual efficient tone.

Amy nodded. "Jo's taken him to the top ring."

"She's not going to get on him without us there, is she?" Mrs. Newhart asked anxiously.

"No, I told her to wait for us," Amy said.

When they got to the top ring, they found Jo massaging Feather's neck with T-touch circles, but instead of standing quietly as he usually did, he was sidestepping and pulling at his reins. "Hi, Mom," Jo said nervously.

"Well, are you going to get on him?" Amy said, going into the ring.

Jo nodded. Taking a deep breath, she pulled down the stirrups and moved around to Feather's left side to mount.

"Don't look so worried," Amy smiled at her reassuringly. She took hold of Feather's snaffle bit to hold him still while Jo mounted.

Shooting an anxious glance at her mom, Jo put her foot in the stirrup.

"Steady, boy," Amy said as Feather sidestepped. He threw his head in the air and backed up. Jo hopped beside him, her left foot still in the stirrup iron.

"Be careful!" Mrs. Newhart called.

"Stand now." Amy soothed Feather. He stood for a moment, giving Jo a chance to spring into the saddle, but as she landed lightly on his back, he plunged forward. Amy hung on.

"Just walk him around," Amy said as Jo fixed her feet in the stirrups. "He'll soon calm down." Although she spoke confidently, inwardly she couldn't help feeling worried. Feather seemed very tense all of a sudden.

Jo touched her heels to Feather's sides. He backed up. Amy clicked her tongue and gave him a slight slap on his flanks. "Go on!" she told him.

Feather jogged forward. Jo pulled him to a walk. "Steady now," she told him, shooting another look in her mom's direction. But Feather continued to jog and pull.

"He is going to be OK with Jo, isn't he?" Lou asked, looking worried, as Amy joined her at the gate.

"Of course," Amy said, trying to sound as if she believed it. She could see that Mrs. Newhart was gripping the top rail of the gate with white knuckles.

Tim moved closer to Amy. "Jo's looking tense," he muttered, his eyes on the horse and rider.

Amy nodded. Jo's shoulders were stiff. As Feather turned the corner at the top end of the ring and began to head toward them, he crabbed sideways, his haunches coming underneath him and his head held high. "Relax, Jo!" Amy called out as Jo tightened her grip on the reins. What was up with Feather? In the two weeks he had been at Heartland he hadn't behaved like this once. Why had he chosen today of all days?

"Maybe you should get off, honey, and let Amy try," Mrs. Newhart called.

"I'm fine, Mom," Jo said. Her face tense, she turned Feather across the center of the ring. When he continued to pull, she looked anxiously at the gate.

"She's got to stop worrying about her mom and just concentrate on riding him," Tim said under his breath to Amy.

It was as if his words had turned on a lightbulb over Amy's head. "Of course!" she exclaimed, staring at her father. "That's it! That's what's the matter!"

"What?" Tim said, looking mystified.

But Amy didn't have time to explain. She had to get Jo off Feather before anything happened. "Jo!" she called, hurrying across the ring. Feather had stopped, his body parallel to the gate. Jo tried to urge him on, but he shook his head and plunged toward the gate, unseating her slightly.

Amy heard Mrs. Newhart gasp.

Amy tried desperately to stay calm. She wanted to shout, but she knew that doing so would risk frightening Feather, and right now that was the last thing she wanted. She saw Jo nudge his sides. With a snort he began to back up, his head held high.

Amy gave up trying to be calm and broke into a run. "Jo! Get off!" she cried.

Chapter Eleven

❧

Amy was too late. Just as she shouted, Jo kicked Feather again and he reared, his front legs striking out into the air.

"Jo-Ann!" Mrs. Newhart screamed.

For one awful moment, Amy saw Feather stagger and thought he was going to go over backward, but then Jo threw her weight forward, and he regained his balance and landed squarely back on the ground.

In an instant Amy had moved in beside him. "Easy now." She soothed him, grabbing the reins. Then, seeing Mrs. Newhart running across the ring toward them, she shot a look at Jo. "Are you OK?"

Jo's face was white, but she nodded.

"Jo-Ann!" Mrs. Newhart yelled as she ran across the ring, her pumps sinking into the sand.

Jo scrambled off Feather's back. "Mom — please."

"Get away from that horse right now," Mrs. Newhart said, hugging her fiercely, her eyes full of fear.

"It's OK, Mom, I'm fine," Jo said.

Mrs. Newhart was almost in tears. "Enough's enough. The pony has to go."

"But Mrs. Newhart," Amy said quickly. "I know what's wrong now. If you'll just give Feather another chance —"

"Another chance!" Mrs. Newhart echoed, looking at her as if she was crazy. "You've got real nerve!" Her voice rose. "You told me he was safe. Jo-Ann could have been killed!"

"If you'll just let me explain," Amy began.

But Mrs. Newhart cut her off. "No!" she said furiously. "I'm through with explanations. Jo-Ann, you're not to go near that pony again!"

"Mom!" Jo protested.

Mrs. Newhart grabbed her arm. "No, Jo. I gave Feather a second chance, but no more," she said, her eyes boring into her daughter's face. "I'm not prepared to let you put yourself in danger anymore. You know what happened to your grandmother. I won't let a horse ruin your life, too. You're coming home with me right now."

"But —"

"I mean it, Jo-Ann," Mrs. Newhart cut in furiously.

"Unless you want me to ban you from even going near horses. Now get into that car!"

Jo seemed to realize that her mom was serious, and sobbing bitterly, she ran down the yard. Her mother strode after her.

"Mrs. Newhart, wait," Lou said, following them.

Amy groaned and buried her head in Feather's neck. He nuzzled her back, and looking up she saw the puzzlement in his eyes. "Well, Feather," she sighed, "you've really gone and done it now." She couldn't believe she hadn't figured out what the problem was sooner. If she had only realized, this whole incident could have been prevented.

"Are you OK?" Tim's voice said.

Amy looked around. Her father was walking across the ring toward her. "No," she said.

"You can't blame yourself," Tim said softly. "You thought he was cured. Everyone did."

Amy shook her head. "Deep down I think I knew that we hadn't really figured out his problem." She kicked the sand in frustration. "If only I'd seen what the matter was sooner, none of this would have happened, and Jo would have been able to keep him."

"So why do you think he reared?" Tim asked.

"I'm sure it's because of Jo," Amy explained. "He's so sensitive — he's reacting to Jo's tension whenever she rides in front of her mom." She shook her head. "She even told me that the only times he misbehaved were when her mom was watching, but I didn't connect that with him rearing. I thought it was just bad luck."

"I think you're right," Tim said, nodding. "Jo's tense because she knows how nervous her mom is. He picks up on that tension and starts getting upset."

"Yes, and he tries to pull to the gate to get out of the ring," Amy continued. "Then when Jo stops him, he panics because he can't escape. He's frightened, so he rears." She patted Feather. "I'm sure that's what's causing it. He's so responsive — it's like he can read your mind. I'm sure he's just reacting to Jo's anxiety when her mom's watching."

"Well, why don't you get on him and see?" Tim said. "If he's good with you now, then it will certainly support the idea that the problem is Jo's tension."

Amy looked at him in surprise. "You'd let me, even after he just reared like that?"

"I wouldn't have thought I could prevent you," Tim said with a wry smile. "Seriously. If I thought you were in any real danger, of course I'd try to stop you, but I agree with your theory."

Amy smiled at him and took hold of Feather's reins. "Here goes," she said, mounting.

Feather stood like a rock as she adjusted the stirrup leathers. Once she was ready, she squeezed his sides. He walked forward calmly. Shortening the reins, Amy walked, trotted, and then cantered three circuits. Feather responded perfectly. To finish, she leaned forward and galloped him down the long side of the ring. As she reached the corner she slowed him to a canter, circled him, and then trotted him over to the gate.

"I'm right. I know I am!" Amy exclaimed, her face glowing.

"Well done," Tim said, looking at her proudly.

As their eyes met, a wave of emotion overwhelmed Amy. *He understands me,* she thought. *He's my father.* As the words repeated in her brain, they were a true comfort to her. She was his daughter, and despite the twelve years that had passed, she knew with a sudden certainty that there was a bond between them that couldn't be broken.

"Oh, Daddy," she exclaimed. "Thank you for helping me understand what was wrong! I couldn't have figured it out without you."

"You called me Daddy," Tim said, looking surprised but delighted.

"Well, that's who you are," Amy replied, her eyes shining. "Thank you."

"I didn't do anything," Tim said. "It was you who took the chance." His gray eyes scanned her face. "Amy, you're a talented person, and I just want to say how proud I am to know you."

Amy had to force the words past the lump that was

swelling in her throat. "Thank you, Daddy," she managed to say, her eyes brimming with tears. "It means a lot to me. It really does."

"Oh, Amy, you'll never know how much it means to me to hear you say that," Tim said.

"It's true," Amy said.

For a moment, they just smiled at each other, but then the sound of footsteps on the gravel path behind them made them turn.

"Lou!" Amy said.

Lou stared at her in horror. "Amy! What are you doing on Feather?" she exclaimed. "Get off!"

The good news burst from Amy. "No, it's fine! I've figured out what was wrong. Feather's safe. He was just reacting to Jo's tension. Watch." She gathered up Feather's reins and squeezed him on.

"No!" Lou gasped.

The intensity in Lou's voice made Amy bring Feather to a halt. "But he's fine."

"Get off now!" Lou's voice rose almost hysterically.

"It's OK, Lou," Tim said. "Amy's just been riding him. There isn't a problem."

Lou rounded on him. "I can't believe you let Amy get on him!"

"I —" Tim began.

"How could you have been so irresponsible?" Lou cried. "Amy could have been seriously injured."

"But she hasn't been," Tim said. "She —"

"So that makes it OK, does it?" Lou exclaimed, interrupting him. Shaking with emotion, she glared furiously at him. "For goodness' sake! You of all people should know how dangerous horses can be. How could you let Amy risk herself that way? Don't you care about her at all?"

"Of course I care," Tim said. "I —" He broke off, and Amy saw a sudden look of comprehension cross his face. "This isn't about Amy, is it, Lou?" he said suddenly. "This is about you."

Lou stared. "What? What are you talking about?"

"All this emotion," Tim said. "This overreaction to Amy riding. I was right — you're scared of horses, aren't you?"

"Don't be ridiculous!" Lou snapped.

Tim shook his head. "I think you are. Oh, Lou, don't let what happened to me affect your life like this. I know I was injured. I know there are risks involved with riding and being around horses — as there are with a lot of things in life. But we have to take chances or else life's not worth anything." His eyes searched hers. "You've got to face this fear, Lou. If you don't, you'll always wonder what might have been."

"Got to!" Lou spat. "How dare you tell me what I've got to do! You lost the right to do that the day you abandoned me!" she said, turning on her heel and marching away.

There was silence. Amy glanced at her father. His face was white. "I'd better go after her," he said.

"No," Amy said quickly. "Let her calm down."

Tim hesitated for a moment and then nodded. "Maybe that would be for the best." He looked at Amy. "But I'm right. This has to do with her fear of riding."

"I know," Amy said, remembering the look of terror in Lou's eyes when she saw that Amy was on Feather. It was the same as the look on Mrs. Newhart's face when she ran across the ring after Feather had reared with Jo. Tim was right. Lou was scared, even if she wouldn't admit it.

Tim sighed. "I shouldn't have said anything. I don't want to leave with things on a bad note between us."

"Just give her a little time," Amy said, hoping she was right. She patted the pony. "Well, I guess I better put Feather back in his stall."

"What are you going to do about him?" Tim asked as he followed her down the yard.

"I don't know," Amy said, forcing her mind to focus on the issue of Feather. "I guess it's really Jo who needs the remedy, not him. Maybe I could try giving her something to help her nerves. Bach Flower Remedies are good for dealing with anxiety. But I just can't see Mrs.

Newhart allowing Jo near Feather again, even if I can get her to listen to me about what's wrong."

"Is there anyone who could help Jo change her mom's mind?" Tim said. "What about the uncle who bought Feather?"

"I could call Jo and ask," Amy said, feeling a glimmer of hope.

"Why not call now? I'll put Feather in his stall," Tim said.

Amy went to the kitchen. There was no sign of Lou anywhere. Picking up the telephone, Amy punched in the Newharts' number. She wondered what she'd say if Mrs. Newhart answered the phone, but to her relief, it was Jo who took the call. Amy quickly explained what she thought the reasons might be behind Feather misbehaving. "Are you sure he's only ever acted up when your mom's been watching?" she asked.

"Oh, Amy!" Jo exclaimed. "I think you're right. Can you tell Mom and persuade her not to sell Feather?"

"I doubt she'll listen to me," Amy said. "But I was wondering if there's anyone else she'll listen to in your family. The uncle who bought Feather, maybe?"

"He's in Canada," Jo said, "on business for the next three months. The only other person in the family who knows about horses is my grandma. Maybe she'll speak to Mom." Jo sounded more hopeful than sure.

"I thought you said that she'd sold all her horses after the accident," Amy said.

"That's right," Jo admitted. "And she doesn't know about Feather. Mom thought it might upset her if she knew I had a horse. We never mention horses when we visit. She's been afraid of them since the accident."

"Well, I don't think it sounds like she'll help," Amy said.

"But she might," Jo said. "Will you try to speak to her, Amy?"

Amy hesitated. "I guess I could try," she said doubtfully.

"Oh, thank you!" Jo cried.

When Amy put the receiver down, she looked at the name and number that Jo had given her. Would this work? Taking a deep breath, she punched in the new number.

❧

Ten minutes later, she put down the phone, wondering whether she had done the right thing. Mary Butler, Jo's grandmother, had sounded very frail, and it had taken Amy quite a long time to explain who she was and what she wanted. However, at last she had gotten Mrs. Butler to agree to come to Heartland and see Feather. Amy hoped that if Mrs. Butler saw Jo riding him, she would realize that he wasn't dangerous and would help persuade Mrs. Newhart to let Jo keep him.

She called Jo again. "Your grandmother's agreed to come and see him later this afternoon," she said.

"That's wonderful!" Jo exclaimed.

"She hasn't said she'll help persuade your mom," Amy said, remembering how little Mrs. Butler had said beyond agreeing—nervously, it seemed — to come to Heartland that afternoon. "But at least she's coming. Can you come over about four o'clock to ride Feather?"

"I can't," Jo said. "Mom's banned me from getting on him again. Oh, Amy, what am I going to do?"

"OK, don't worry, Jo. We'll find a way to work this out," Amy said quickly, half believing it herself.

✍

After she got off the phone, Amy went to finish the yard chores with her dad and Ben. She had hoped that an opportunity would come up for her dad to talk with Lou and work things out. Just before lunchtime, however, she saw Lou get into her car and drive away.

"Where's Lou gone?" she asked, bursting into the kitchen where Grandpa was sitting, reading the local paper.

"Lunch with Scott," Grandpa replied.

"But it's Daddy's last day here!" Amy exclaimed.

"Yes, I thought it was a little odd," Grandpa said. "But

she seemed determined to go." He saw Amy's face fall. "Has something happened?"

"Not really," Amy said, not wanting him to worry. "It's nothing." She went back to the yard. Nothing. Their father was leaving in three hours. What if Lou wasn't back by then?

Chapter Twelve

Three hours later, Lou still hadn't returned.

"Well, I have to go," Tim said to Amy. "I need to pack and check out of the hotel."

"But you can't go without saying good-bye to Lou," Amy protested.

"Believe me, I don't want to," Tim said, looking at his watch. "But I don't have much choice if I want to catch my plane home."

Suddenly, there was the sound of a car coming up the drive. "It's Lou!" Amy exclaimed with relief.

It was. Lou parked and got out.

"Daddy's just leaving," Amy told her.

As she spoke, Grandpa came out of the house. "So you're going?" he said to Tim.

"That's right, Jack," Tim replied. He looked awkwardly at Lou. "Lou —"

Lou marched to Jack's side. "Bye, Daddy," she said, her voice abrupt.

Amy saw her father glance at Jack, and her heart sank. She knew there was no way he was going to get into a heavy talk with Lou when Grandpa was standing there. Her thoughts raced as she tried to figure out how she could get Grandpa out of the way for a few moments. But it was too late. Grandpa held out his hand.

"Good-bye, Tim," he said. "Thank you for coming. Truly."

Amy saw her dad's shoulders sag slightly. "Good-bye, Jack," he said, stepping forward to shake hands, and Amy knew then that he had given up hope of making things right with Lou. "Thank you for allowing me to visit." He turned to Amy. "Bye, sweetheart," he said, hugging her tight. "Promise you'll come and stay with me sometime."

"I promise," Amy said, feeling tears springing to her eyes. After wishing for so long that he wouldn't come and visit, now she didn't want him to leave, particularly not with everything feeling so unresolved. "And I'll phone and e-mail you."

Tim kissed the top of her head. "You'd better. After all, I want to know what happens when Mary Butler visits."

"Mary Butler?" Grandpa said.

"Jo's grandmother," Amy explained. "She's coming this afternoon. I'm hoping that if I can show her Feather's not dangerous" — she glanced at Lou, who looked away quickly — "then she'll help me persuade Mrs. Newhart to let Jo keep him." She saw Grandpa raise his eyebrows. "I know it's a long shot, but I've got to try something."

"I really hope it works," Tim said. He hugged her once more, and then, letting her go, he turned to Lou.

"Lou?" he said holding out his hands. Lou's jaw clenched, and for a moment Amy thought she was going to ignore their father's outstretched hands. But then she walked briskly forward. They hugged briefly, her body stiff. "Have a safe trip," she said.

Her voice was cool and polite, and there were signs of strain around her eyes and mouth. *Just say that you'll miss him, Lou,* Amy thought desperately. But Lou didn't. Moving back beside Grandpa, she watched as Tim got into his car and started the engine.

"Bye," he said, lowering the window. "Get in touch soon." Amy could see the sadness in his eyes, and she felt a lump of tears in her throat. "Bye, Daddy," she said, swallowing hard.

He drove off.

For a moment no one spoke, and then Lou turned and ran into the house.

Amy moved to go after her, but Grandpa stopped her.

"Lou's got some issues to deal with, Amy. She needs time on her own."

"I just don't get her," Amy said in frustration. "She didn't say she'd miss him or anything. She hardly even hugged him."

"I know," Jack said gently. "Maybe next time he visits things will be easier."

Next time, Amy thought as he went back into the house. *Who knows when that will be?*

She kicked a loose stone. Feeling miserable, she walked to Feather's stall to give him a last brushing before Jo's grandmother arrived.

❧

At five minutes to four, a minivan came up the driveway. An old woman with silver hair was driving. As she parked, Amy walked over, butterflies fluttering in her stomach. What was Mrs. Butler going to be like? If her family had never mentioned horses around her since the accident, was she really going to be interested in helping? Amy groaned inwardly. Was this all just a huge mistake?

The door opened. "Hello," Amy said. "I'm Amy Fleming."

"Mary Butler," the woman said, a nervous quaver to her voice. "Pleased to meet you." They shook hands. Mrs. Butler looked just a few years older than Grandpa, but very frail. "Would you be so kind as to get my wheel-chair out of the back?" she said in a low, shaky voice.

"Of course," Amy said. As she opened the back door, she noticed that the minivan was specially adapted. The back had no seats, just Mrs. Butler's wheelchair. She brought it out and helped Mrs. Butler into it.

"Thank you," the woman said. She looked around the yard, and for a moment Amy had the impression that her eyes had the look of someone who was trapped, some-one who wanted to flee.

Amy's heart sank. This was a bad, bad idea. Mrs. But-ler was never going to be able to help. Just then, the back door opened, and to Amy's surprise, Lou came out. "Hello," she said, walking over to Mrs. Butler. "I'm Lou Fleming, Amy's sister."

For one nightmare moment, Amy wondered whether Lou was about to launch into a speech about how dan-gerous Feather was. But she didn't. She just smiled. "Would you like to take a look around the place?"

Mary Butler hesitated and took a deep breath. "Yes. That would be nice," she whispered.

As Lou moved behind the wheelchair and took hold of the handles, Amy saw that her eyes were red. It looked as if she'd been crying. However, she couldn't question her sister at that moment. Lou seemed to be unaware of Amy's stare as she wheeled Jo's grandmother over to the turnout paddocks and then to the stable block. She pointed out each of the horses in turn. Wondering why she was helping, Amy decided to follow her.

As Lou chatted about the horses, saying their names and a little about them, Jo's grandmother visibly seemed to relax. Seeing this, Amy stopped worrying about why Lou was helping and just felt relieved.

"This is Red and Rosie and Jake," Lou said pointing out each horse as she spoke. Red and Rosie were spooked by the wheelchair, but Jake bent his great bay head and snuffled at Mrs. Butler's hair.

"Jake! Manners!" Amy said, moving quickly to push the big horse back.

"It's — it's OK," Mary Butler said. "I don't mind." With trembling fingers, she reached into her coat pocket and pulled out a mint candy. "Here, boy," she murmured, holding it out on the flat of her hand. "I think this is what you're looking for."

Always eager for treats, Jake gently lipped the candy up. Jo's grandmother sat as if transfixed. Crunching happily, Jake lifted his muzzle to her face, and the woman stroked his nose gently with her hand.

"Thirty years," she said, her voice so low that Amy almost didn't catch it. She glanced around at Amy and Lou. "This is the first time I've touched a horse in thirty years."

Even Lou seemed at a loss for words at this revelation.

"I take it you know about my accident?" Mary Butler said.

Amy and Lou nodded.

"And so you know that after it, I let all my horses be sold? My four beautiful horses."

Amy frowned at the word "let." "But I thought you wanted to sell them."

Mrs. Butler shook her head. "Every time my husband or my daughter even looked at a horse I knew they were reminded of what they no longer had — a healthy wife, a fit mother."

"So you gave up your horses?" Lou said.

Mrs. Butler nodded. "I got rid of everything to do with horses. The stables were turned into a garage, my horse pictures and trophies were put in the trash, even my jodhpurs were given away."

Amy was stunned. If she'd have known that Jo's grandmother had put such a distance between herself and horses, she would never have called her.

Lou looked curious. "So why did you agree to come here today?"

"I don't know," Mrs. Butler said. "I think it was just the push I needed. My husband — Jo-Ann's grandfather — died last year, and since then I've been wondering whether what I did was right or misguided." She reached out to touch Jake's nose again. "And now I know," she said. "Seeing these horses, smelling them, touching them. How could I have shut all these sensations from my life? I made a big mistake — a terrible mistake." Her voice shook on the last word. "For thirty years, I've denied myself something that could have given me so much happiness. What a stupid woman I've been."

Amy glanced at Lou and saw that her sister's face looked thoughtful.

The old woman shook her head. "I don't want Jo-Ann to suffer in the same way. Now where is her pony? I want to see him."

"He's in the back barn," Amy said.

Lou didn't say a word as she pushed the wheelchair to the barn.

"So you're the fella who's been causing all sorts of trouble?" Mrs. Butler said when they introduced her to Feather. "You're certainly a handsome boy."

"Grandma!" They all turned. Jo was running down the aisle toward them.

"What are you doing here, Jo?" Amy said.

"I know I can't ride Feather," Jo said breathlessly, "but I had to see my grandma and tell her how wonderful my pony is. I wrote Mom a note saying I'd come back here to get my jacket and I'd be home soon. Please, Grandma," she said, stopping by her grandmother's chair, "you've got to help. Feather's not dangerous." She suddenly seemed to notice that the old woman was patting Feather's neck. "Aren't you afraid of him?" she exclaimed.

"I've never been afraid of a horse in my life, honey," Mary Butler said, smiling. "I've just kept away from them. But I'm beginning to realize how much I have lost." She took Jo's hand. "And I don't want to see you miss out in the same way. Let me watch you ride your pony, and if he is safe like Amy says, then I'll do everything in my power to persuade your mom to let you keep him."

"Oh, Grandma, thank you!" Jo gasped. She looked worried. "But Mom said I wasn't to ride him."

Mrs. Butler squeezed her hand. "Don't worry. I'll take the blame."

❧

Ten minutes later, Feather was tacked up. "Now before you get on, put a few drops of this on your tongue," Amy said, handing Jo a small brown bottle.

"What is it?" Jo peered at the label. "Agrimony? What's that?"

"It's a Bach Flower Remedy," Amy explained. "It will help to release any tension you're feeling and will help you to relax. It's a natural mixture we sometimes use on horses."

Jo took the remedy and then led Feather up to the school. Amy joined Lou and Mrs. Butler at the gate.

"Just stay calm," Amy told Jo as she mounted.

"I will," Jo said. And she did. Whether it was the remedy or the fact that she knew why Feather had been misbehaving or the knowledge that she had her grandmother's support, Amy couldn't tell. All that mattered was that Jo relaxed into the saddle, and Feather behaved like a dream.

"See, Grandma!" Jo said triumphantly as she finally brought him to a stop by the gate. "Isn't he perfect?"

"He is," Mary Butler said quietly. She turned to Amy. "You know, you're a very remarkable young woman to figure out what was wrong with this pony and then to go to the lengths of contacting me. Thank you."

"So will you try to persuade Mom to let me keep him, Grandma?" Jo asked.

Her grandmother nodded. "I most certainly will." The pinched look had left her face, and a happy flush of color now suffused her cheekbones. "And I'll also tell her that I intend to start riding again myself." She smiled. "I may be seventy, but there's still a good few years left in me, and I want to make up for lost time."

Jo's face lit up. "Grandma, that's fantastic! We could go riding together." She patted Feather's neck. "Oh, Feather, do you hear that — isn't it the best news?"

"Jo-Ann!" The half scream, half shout made them all swing around.

There, on the path, was Mrs. Newhart coming toward them. She was staring at Jo and Feather with shock in her eyes.

Chapter Thirteen

"What on earth do you think you are doing, Jo?" Mrs. Newhart cried, her face turning pale. She started to run toward them. "I saw your note and knew you'd be doing something like this. Thank goodness I came. Get off that pony right now!"

"Donna, stop it!"

Mrs. Newhart stopped in her tracks, and for the first time her gaze took in the figure in the wheelchair, half hidden behind Lou and Amy. "Mom?" she said in astonishment. "What are you doing here?"

"I'm here because Amy called me up and told me about Jo-Ann's pony." Mrs. Butler looked at Jo. "Maybe you'd better dismount for a moment, Jo, while we explain things to your mom." As Jo dismounted, Mrs. Butler shook her head. "Why didn't you tell me what was happening, Donna?" she said to Mrs. Newhart.

Mrs. Newhart's eyes flickered from Mrs. Butler to Jo. She looked as if she didn't know what to do first — yell at Jo or answer Mrs. Butler's question.

"You should have told me about Feather," Mrs. Butler said to her.

"I — I didn't want to upset you, Mother," Mrs. Newhart said. "I know how much you hate horses."

"Hate them?" Mrs Butler said. "I've always loved horses, Donna. I only gave them up because I didn't want to upset you and your father."

"So you're not scared of them?" Mrs. Newhart said falteringly.

"No," Mrs. Butler replied. "Not at all."

"But even after everything that happened — the horse falling on you —"

"It was an accident," Mrs. Butler said. "The horse wasn't to blame, Donna. It couldn't have stopped the fall any more than I could." She sighed. "I know how much it affected you, but please, don't let it blight Jo-Ann's life, too. Of course you should protect her, but not at the expense of her happiness. Feather isn't a dangerous pony. I've been watching him. He and Jo have a wonderful bond. You should let her keep him."

Mrs. Newhart looked at a loss for words.

Lou quickly spoke up. "Your mother's right, Mrs. Newhart," she said. "Jo loves riding, and if you try to stop her, she'll always wonder what might have been. There are risks when you work with horses, but there are risks in anything in life that is worthwhile."

Amy stared as she recognized their father's words from earlier, but Lou avoided her sister's gaze.

Mrs. Newhart nodded slowly. "You're right," she sighed. "I know you are. But" — her eyes glanced anxiously at Feather — "is he really safe? I mean, earlier, when he reared —"

"Amy can explain his behavior," Mrs. Butler said. She looked at Amy, who quickly took her cue and explained why Feather had been acting up.

"I see," Mrs. Newhart said slowly as Amy finished. "So it was because Feather was worried about Jo and trying to protect her. He could tell she wasn't happy?"

"Yes," Amy said, nodding. "He's a very sensitive pony, and he loves Jo very much."

"Please can I keep him, Mom?" Jo burst out.

Mrs. Newhart took a deep breath. "All right, Jo-Ann," she said. "I want you to be happy. Provided he continues to behave, you can keep him."

"Oh, Mom!" Jo cried. Flinging the reins at Amy, she raced across the sand and threw her arms around her mom. "Thank you! Thank you so much!"

✖

Half an hour later, Jo, her mom, and Mrs. Butler left, with Jo chatting happily about how she was going to help her grandmother learn to ride again.

"I've never seen Jo so happy," Amy said as she and Lou waved good-bye to them.

"I'm really pleased for her," Lou said quietly. "And for Feather." She wandered over to the nearby paddock fence and leaned against it with a sigh.

"What's up?" Amy said, joining her.

"I had some news this morning," Lou said. She looked across the paddock. The evening shadows were just starting to lengthen across the grass, and the last rays of the sun fell on the grazing shapes of Dancer and Solo. "I've been trying to find the right moment to tell you. We didn't get the land."

"We didn't?" Amy said, frowning. "Who did? Green Briar?"

"No, don't worry," Lou answered her quickly. "The Youngs have decided not to sell."

"Not to sell?" Amy looked puzzled. "You mean they've pulled out of the deal?"

"Yeah, they're going to extend their farm and try to make things work for themselves," Lou shrugged.

"Oh, Lou." Amy touched her sister's arm sympathetically. "I'm sorry. I know it meant a lot to you."

Lou stared out at the horses for a moment. "It did," she admitted. "But I've been thinking about it since lunchtime, and I think it might be for the best. If I'm honest, I guess I wanted it to happen not so much because it would be the ideal thing for Heartland but because I hoped it would make me feel more important. It would have been my very own project — something for me to work on and to shape." She glanced at Amy. "You, Grandpa, Ty — you all have your own roles here. I don't."

"But you do!" Amy protested in astonishment. "We couldn't run the business side of things without you."

"You could," Lou said sadly. "You could get someone else to do the accounts and marketing. You could hire an administrator."

"But they wouldn't have your ideas," Amy told her. "And anyway, it's not just the business side of things that we need you for. You're good at talking to people — much better than I am or than any of us are. You were the one who persuaded Mrs. Newhart to let Feather come to Heartland in the first place, and this afternoon you were the one who made Mrs. Butler feel at ease and helped make Mrs. Newhart understand why Jo should be allowed to keep Feather."

Lou looked slightly surprised. "I did?"

"Yes!" A question that had been lurking at the back of

Amy's mind rose to her lips. "But what I don't get is why you came out to help when Mrs. Butler arrived. I mean this morning you made it pretty clear that you thought Feather was dangerous."

"I know." Lou hesitated. "But I — I talked that over with Scott at lunchtime, and he pointed out that Daddy wouldn't have let you ride Feather if he'd thought that the horse was dangerous. He made me realize that I'd overreacted."

"So why didn't you say anything to Daddy before he left?" Amy said, frowning. "He was really upset, Lou."

Lou didn't reply.

"Lou," Amy said, remembering the hurt in their father's eyes as he'd left, "you should have said something. You should have talked to him. He didn't want to leave things on such a bad note with you. He wanted to work things out. He —"

The words "loves you" froze on her lips as she saw Lou's shoulders suddenly shake.

"Oh, Amy!" The words burst from Lou in a sob. "I wanted to. I know I should have made up. But I felt so mad at him I just couldn't do it."

"But why?" Amy said, bewildered.

"Why?" Lou turning on her. "Why do you think? All week it's been you and Daddy doing this, you and Daddy doing that. Well, what about me?"

Amy stared. "You could have done things with Daddy, too, but you didn't want to. You just kept working inside."

"He could have come in and seen me."

"But you kept saying you were busy!" Amy exclaimed. "Lou, you can't blame him for not disturbing you when you told him you were working. That's not fair!"

"I know, I know." Lou bowed her head. "I'm sorry," she said quietly. "It wasn't your fault, Amy, or Daddy's. It was mine. I just had this whole big idea in my head of what Daddy's visit would be like. You know, running up the drive and throwing my arms around him — all that stuff that you see in the movies — but it wasn't like that. Daddy's changed so much."

Amy hesitated. "Are you sure it's Daddy who's changed, Lou?" she said tentatively. "Not you? After all" — she paused, wondering how to put her thoughts into words without offending Lou — "not liking horses anymore is a major difference."

"It's not that I don't like them," Lou said. "It's just — just —"

Amy wanted to finish Lou's sentence, but something told her that the words had to come from her sister. "Just what?" she prompted.

"I'm scared of them," Lou whispered. She swallowed, her eyes meeting Amy's. "Daddy was right. I am afraid. Oh, I don't mind handling them," she said, seeing Amy's expression. "It's just riding them. Whenever I think about getting on one, all I can see in my mind is the picture of Daddy falling and Pegasus crumpling down." Fresh sobs tore through her. "I was there that night. I watched it happen, and I've never forgotten it. That's why I avoided Daddy. He knew, and I couldn't face him. He's always been so brave. I couldn't bear for him to think of me as a coward."

Amy touched her sister's back. "It's OK," she murmured. "It'll be all right, Lou."

Lou raised her tear-streaked face. "How?" she demanded. "You can't change the past."

"No, but we can move on," Amy said. "Remember what Daddy said. You can't let what happened to him ruin your life, but if you don't face your fears, it will. You can't shut horses out of your life, not when you used to love them so much. You saw how much Jo's grandmother regrets it."

"I know," Lou whispered. "But Amy, I just can't get on one. I can't."

Amy thought quickly. If she was dealing with a frightened horse, what would she do? *Take things slowly of course,* she thought. *One step at a time.*

"So don't start by riding," she said. "Just start working one from the ground." An idea grew in her mind. "Join up, Lou. You could try to join up with one of the horses."

"No, it wouldn't work," Lou began, shaking her head.

"Yes, it would," Amy insisted. She glanced out the barn door. It was dusk but not quite evening yet. "You could do it now, Lou."

"Now?" Lou echoed.

"Yes, with" — Amy thought quickly — "with Sugarfoot," she said.

❧

Ten minutes later, Lou was reluctantly standing in the middle of the ring with Amy. "I'm really not sure about this," she said.

"You'll be fine," Amy said, wishing she could give some of her own confidence to Lou. She unclipped the little Shetland's lead rope and patted his chestnut back. "He hasn't joined up with anyone before, but I'm sure he'll be fine."

Looking rather surprised to be in the ring, Sugarfoot wandered away, his muzzle to the sand, his thick flaxen mane flopping over his neck. "Just remember, keep your shoulders square and your eyes on his," Amy said, starting to go toward the gate.

"Aren't you going to stay with me?" Lou asked anxiously.

"It'll be easier for you if I'm not there," Amy said. "You need to just concentrate on Sugarfoot, listen to the signals he's giving you, and respond to them."

She climbed over the gate. The sun had dropped below the horizon, and the shadows around the ring were lengthening. In the tall trees behind the ring, a single bird sang softly in the evening light. Amy leaned against the gate, her eyes on her sister. Lou was standing in the center of the ring, moving the rope rather nervously from hand to hand.

It took all of Amy's willpower not to shout out an instruction. But she knew that this was something Lou had to figure out on her own.

Rather awkwardly, Lou flicked the end of the long line toward Sugarfoot. He looked at her in surprise and trotted a few paces before slowing again and stopping to snuff at the ground. She clicked her tongue and pitched the rope at his hindquarters. Sugarfoot swung around and looked at her.

Amy gripped the gate. "Eyes, Lou, eyes!" she muttered.

As if she had heard, Lou fixed her eyes on the chestnut Shetland and squared her shoulders with his. This time when she pitched the rope, Sugarfoot broke into a trot, and then, as Lou moved the rope toward him again, into a canter, his short legs pounding around the ring.

Seeming to grow in confidence with every circuit he made, Lou kept him going, working him around the ring, then changing direction and sending him on again.

"There!" Amy whispered as Sugarfoot made the tiniest movement with his mouth. Soon he was chewing and licking, and his head started stretching down. Amy glanced at Lou's face. It was utterly focused on the little Shetland. Suddenly, she turned her shoulders in. Sugarfoot stopped within a few strides, and then with hardly a hesitation he walked straight across the ring to where Lou was standing, her eyes on the ground, her back to him. With a snort he stopped behind her and nuzzled her back.

"Way to go, Lou!" Amy whispered, smiling broadly as Lou turned to the pony and rubbed his forehead, just as Amy herself would have done.

Remembering to walk away, Lou set off across the ring. Sugarfoot walked after her. Wherever Lou went, the little Shetland followed like a shadow. At last Lou stopped.

"Lou! You did it!" Amy cried, unable to contain her delight any longer.

Lou's face lit up with an ecstatic grin as Amy scrambled over the gate. "I did! I really did!"

As Amy reached her, she flung her arms around Amy, and they hugged each other. When Lou drew back, her eyes were shining. "Oh, Amy, it was the most wonderful, amazing thing!"

"I know," Amy said, grinning.

Lou's face glowed. It was as if all her earlier tension

and unhappiness had been completely wiped away. "It felt like magic — the feeling I got when he came up to me!" Her voice bubbled with emotion. "It was like electricity. Suddenly, I felt I could —"

"Speak his language," Amy said.

Lou nodded. "That's it exactly!" She ran a hand through her hair. "Oh, wow!" she said, grinning from ear to ear. "I almost feel as if I could get on a horse and ride right now."

"Another day," Amy said, knowing how important it was to just take one day at a time.

Lou nodded. "Yes, you're right." She patted Sugarfoot and grinned joyfully at Amy. "Oh, wow. I don't think I'm ever going to come down to earth."

A familiar male voice called through the growing darkness. "Why try?"

Amy and Lou swung around.

"Daddy!" They both gasped, staring at their father, who had stepped out of the shadows at the side of the ring.

"I couldn't leave with things the way they were," Tim said, opening the gate and coming across the ring toward them. "I was on my way to the airport when I decided to stop by. I went to the house, and Jack said you were both here."

"Did you see Lou joining up?" Amy asked eagerly.

"I certainly did." Tim smiled. "I saw it all."

"You were right, Daddy," Lou said. "I didn't want to admit it, but I was scared."

"And what about now?" Tim asked, watching her closely.

"Not so much," Lou said. "And maybe" — she took a deep breath — "maybe when you visit next time I won't be scared at all."

"Lou, I'm so proud of you," Tim said softly. "I know how hard it is to face up to your fears. I was so afraid of getting in contact with the two of you again that I put it off again and again. It was only your persistence that made me get in touch again. I lost twelve years of your lives, but it could have been so many more."

Lou looked a little embarrassed. "I wish I had spent more time with you this week."

"It's OK," Tim said. "I know it was hard. We've all had some adjusting to do. At first I didn't know what to say when I saw you — my little girl — grown into a confident, successful young woman with a life and career of her own."

"And a fear of horses," Lou put in.

Tim shook his head. "I never meant to upset you about that. I just couldn't bear the thought of you wasting years of your life by giving into your fear — doing what I did, basically. I just wanted you to be happy. That's all I've ever wanted for both of you." He looked from Amy to Lou. "I know I can't take back the pain I've caused you in the past. But I want you to know that if you ever need me, I'll be there for you. I accept that after everything I've done, I've lost the right to call myself your father. But I would really like it" — he paused — "if we could be friends."

"You'll always be more than that to us," Amy said, going over to hug him.

Lou followed her. "Amy's right. You're our daddy, and nothing can ever change that."

Amy saw the emotion in her father's eyes as he gathered them both into his arms. "My daughters," he murmured into their hair. "My two wonderful daughters."

They hugged for another moment, and then Lou pulled back.

"There's something else I need to tell you, Daddy," she said. "It's about the land. We didn't get it. There isn't going to be a riding school."

"Oh, Lou, I'm sorry," Tim said, looking at her sympathetically. "I know how much you wanted it."

"It's OK," Lou answered. "I'm not sure I wanted it for the right reasons. I think I just wanted to feel important." She glanced at Amy. "But Amy's made me realize that I *am* important here at Heartland — I *do* belong. And if we need to think of a way to raise more funds, well" — she grinned — "I'm never short of money-making ideas."

"That's my girl," Tim said. "And I want to hear all about your plans next time we meet. But right now," he added reluctantly, "I'm going to have to go or I'll miss my plane. We'll see each other again soon?" He made it into a question.

Lou smiled through her tears. "After all the trouble I went to to track you down, you don't think that I'm going to let you lose touch with us again, do you?"

Amy grinned. "You'll have go much farther than Australia if you want to escape from Lou, Daddy."

"Heck!" Tim said with a mock frown. "And I thought I was safe over there." He smiled at Amy. "Don't you stop taking chances, you hear?"

"I don't think there's any danger of that," Lou said wryly.

"And next time I see you," Tim said, turning to her, "maybe we'll all go out on the trails together."

Lou smiled. "I'd like that more than anything else in the world."

Looking at her sister's face, Amy suddenly remembered the old photograph of Lou sitting on her pony. Now joyful and delighted — just as she had been in the photo — Lou seemed a very different person from the one Amy had comforted in the barn just a short time ago.

"I'd better go," Tim said. "And just remember, Lou. You are needed and you *do* belong — here at Heartland, and with me and Amy, too."

He kissed them both on the forehead and patted Sugarfoot. Then with one last look, the tall figure disappeared into the darkness.

"It's getting late," Lou said softly as the night closed around them. "We should go in."

Sugarfoot snorted. As Amy moved to pat him, she saw her sister's hand move toward the pony, too.

Their eyes met. Lou smiled and stroked Sugarfoot's neck. "You know, I think we're a family again, Amy — a real family."

*Share the Moments with Amy
in the next* **Heartland** *title:*

Every New Day

🐎

"I just don't get it," Ben said, looking at Mercury. "Plenty of show horses get rapped. It's not against the rules, as long as they only use a bamboo cane. And it's not all that painful for the horse — the idea is that the trainer just taps the horse's forelegs as he goes over the jump to make him think he's clipped the fence. It only stings a little bit. And the horse learns to jump tighter and higher. I don't understand why Mercury's so wound up."

Amy looked up and saw the frustration on Ben's face.

"I guess they must have used more than a cane on him," she said. "And it's not like it's just a physical thing, anyway. Somehow, they've broken his will to jump."

"I don't think a horse like Mercury ever loses the will to jump," said Ben passionately. "He's born for it. You can just see it in him. He's a real competitor."

Amy sighed and concentrated on the T-touch circles. Somehow, what Ty had said to her earlier kept repeating in her mind. *Mercury will never compete again.* But in her heart, Amy agreed with Ben. They certainly wouldn't

find a solution to Mercury's problem by giving up —
they had to find another way forward.

"Look," she said to Ben. "Let's do a session with him
together tomorrow, when I get in from school, and see
how he goes. We'll try some different techniques."

Ben looked relieved. "Sounds good to me," he said.
"See you later."

He straightened up and left Amy to finish off the session. Amy felt anxious. She could sense that Ben really
wanted to get somewhere with Mercury. It was only natural — Mercury was the first horse he'd really worked
with since coming to Heartland. If they didn't succeed in
curing him, he'd take it personally. That's what Ben was
like. He needed to win to feel good about himself, and
Amy knew he wanted to win with Mercury too.

❧

"It's not working, Ben," Amy called from where she was
perched on the training ring fence. "Take him up to the
top end of the ring again."

Mercury had just refused a small jump made of several bales of straw. The sleek gray horse was backing
away from the makeshift fence, his head in the air and
his eyes rolling. Ben nodded, and guided Mercury back
to the top area of the ring, which was clear of any jumps
or obstacles.

The idea had been to break Mercury's association between poles and jumping. Ben suggested that they introduce Mercury to some nontraditional fences, like the straw, so that the horse wouldn't think of the poles that had rapped his legs. If they could break that connection in Mercury's mind the horse might learn to love jumping again.

Amy had agreed that it was worth a try, but it hadn't worked. "I think we should finish up," she called. "Give him ten more minutes on the lunge, so that he finishes on a good note."

"OK," said Ben in a resigned voice. "I'll come find you when I'm done."

Amy climbed down from the fence and started walking slowly up to the yard. She hated the expression of disappointment and frustration on Ben's face . . . but there was nothing she could do about it. She didn't have any answers. Nothing she had tried with Mercury had worked, either. Ben's idea had been a good one — it made perfect sense. It wasn't his fault that it hadn't worked, but it was clear that he didn't see it that way.

"Amy . . ." Ty's voice broke through her thoughts. "Can you give me a hand moving some sacks of grain?"

Amy nodded. "Sure," she said following him to the feed room.

"So Ben's working Mercury?" asked Ty, grasping a sack firmly.

"Yeah," Amy replied. "But there's still no progress.

Mercury's not responding, and Ben's blaming himself. He thinks it's his fault."

"Well, maybe it is," said Ty evenly. "Maybe he's taking the wrong approach."

"Ty!" protested Amy. "He discusses everything he does with me first. He suggests all the things that we have been trying. Ben has great ideas."

"I don't mean it like that," said Ty. "I just think that it's useless to keep pointing Mercury at fences when he doesn't want to jump."

"But that's why he's here," insisted Amy. "If we just avoid the jumping issue, we're avoiding the problem and we won't be able to cure Mercury."

"Well, maybe he doesn't need to be cured," said Ty irritably.

"What do you mean by that?" Amy said in disbelief. She and Ty had never disagreed about a horse's treatment. Amy had never been so confused — and yet she was sure she was right.

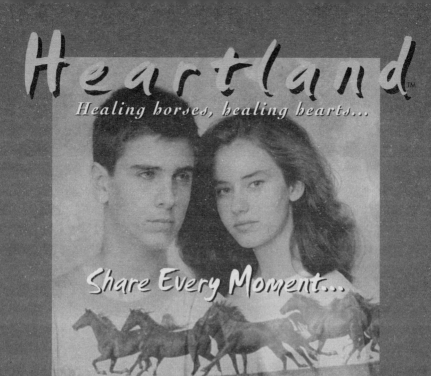